Lett

Letting Go

HAZEL WHITEHEAD

© Hazel Whitehead, 2024

Published by Alvide Publishing

A CIP catalogue record for this book is available from the British Library.

ISBN 978-1-9989930-1-7

Book layout and cover design by Clare Brayshaw

Cover image dreamstime.com

Prepared and printed by:

York Publishing Services Ltd
64 Hallfield Road
Layerthorpe
York YO31 7ZQ

Tel: 01904 431213

Website: www.yps-publishing.co.uk

For Nick, with whom I have shared ministry in diverse ways for fifty years, for our boys who had to grow up with not one inconvenient clergy-parent but two, and for their families.

Contents

Preface

When women and men are ordained in the Church of England, the bishop gives a powerful and weighty address which would scare the bravest souls, if they weren't already terrified. Deacons are to search out the poor and weak, the sick and lonely and those who are oppressed and powerless. . . Priests are to be messengers, watchmen and stewards of the Lord. . . to search for his children in the wilderness of this world's temptations. . . No pressure there, then. Maybe they could fit in a part-time job in the evenings or pull pints in a pub at weekends. If you are tempted to sign up, you can read more at www.churchofengland.org/prayer-and-worship/ worship-texts-and-resources Words like poor and weak, sick and lonely have diverse meanings. Poverty is not only financial, sickness is not only physical and the oppressed and powerless can be found anywhere in the world. Ministry is a big ask. Clergy are, after all, simply women and men doing their best. Revd Bethan Davies, our protagonist, wasn't naïve enough to believe ministry would be easy. She wasn't expecting crowds to flock through the doors of St Jude's and hang on her every word. She both succeeds and fails in her ministry. In this, she is no different from any other vicar. Those she is sent to serve tell stories that are sometimes too painful to bear and her own issues of faith, identity and sexuality (for it's still not easy being a gay member of the Church) complicate matters. She is forced to reframe her understanding of who she is and what God is like by letting go of the images and beliefs she has outgrown. This novel has emerged from encounters and incidents from my ministry as a priest in the Church of England. However, they are not verbatim accounts, accurate reports or witness statements so if you think you recognise yourself or somebody else, you probably don't!

1. The Oak Tree

The weight of Dominic's long-buried secret hung heavily. It disturbed his mind, his body, his soul. Sometimes he felt as if his heart was being squeezed by the world's strongest man – the one with an unpronounceable Scandinavian name and muscles the size of a toddler. It was worse in the early hours when sleep eluded him and he tossed and turned until the light of day seeped through the crack in the curtains.

Daytime was easier. He knew he was a good man because people told him so. He wanted to believe them because he wasn't sure himself. Every day, he was trying to make amends, bringing people closer to one another and more in touch with God; but they didn't know who he was and what he'd done. Right now, he was fine. Monday morning. A new week. Yesterday's services had gone well, and the teenagers had been their usual boisterous selves last night, leaving the floury evidence of their pizza-making behind them. He smiled to himself at their vulnerability and the way they tried to hide it behind masks of confidence. They didn't fool him for one minute.

As he mused, he crammed three casserole dishes into the oven. The ancient gas cooker had a mind of its own so, as usual, he ignored instructions about timings and temperature and hoped for the best. If he turned the oven on now, the meat might be cooked by supper time. As he fiddled with the knob, he stared out of the window and marvelled at the changing colours of the leaves on the ancient oak, the tree which provided privacy, which gave him shade and space to sit away from the public gaze. He loved that oak tree. God had made plants and trees on the third day. They must have meant a lot to him. This tree, his tree, was a symbol of God's faithfulness. It stood there day after day, year after year, spreading its roots further and further into solid ground. It was everything he aspired to be but would never attain. The subdued, autumnal sun glancing off the reds, yellows, and browns reminded him of the stained-glass window in St Jude's, the one where Jesus is laying his hand on a child's head and the boy is looking up with adoration in his eyes.

Dominic loved nothing more than a crowd of parishioners squashing around the scratched, refectory table sharing food and bonhomie. His kitchen cupboards were packed with mismatched tumblers and what his mother called 'church hall green' crockery. Come to think of it, she'd said, that would make a good name for an expensive paint, wouldn't it? There was Rectory Red and Drawing Room Blue. Why not Crockery Green? Not that he would ever buy paint himself. His rectory hadn't been decorated in twenty years but he wasn't going to invite attention by going cap in hand to the diocesan property manager.

One day, he told himself, when the old and the young, the sick and the depressed didn't need his attention, he might have a good spring clean and strip off the swirly wallpaper in the living room himself. Maybe he would have a spring clean, burn all the outdated papers, take his robes to the dry cleaners and hang them up on proper hangers. He could return everything to its rightful place. Or maybe he wouldn't. He rather liked the image he'd cultivated of a godly man living amid holy chaos. However, he must clear the garage and the garden shed which were overflowing with outdated relics of personal and parish life. 'Could be a dead body in here and we'd never know,' his Warden had quipped when they were hunting for the tombola drum last summer.

He began to clear the table. There would be precious little time as the day wore on. Swan Meadows assembly at nine-fifteen, the St. Jude's Flower Festival Committee at eleven-thirty, closely followed by a trustee meeting. Then there were two wedding couples to fit in before Evening Prayer and finally the Oberammergau planning meeting, accompanied by casserole.

He moved the bibles left by the ladies' study group onto a side table and swept aside a week's correspondence. He would deal with it all tomorrow. He turned to his computer and signed on for the final safeguarding module which the Archdeacon had told him he was obliged to do on pain of death. Then took up his fountain pen and made notes for tonight's meeting. Eighteen parishioners had signed up for next year's passion play, and urgent decisions had to be made. A five-and-a-half-hour performance in German, albeit including a three-hour interval, was a tough call. He wanted to be sure they knew precisely what they were letting themselves in for, including the all-too-realistic crucifixion scene. Dominic was nothing if not sensitive to the emotions of other people. No. That wasn't the whole truth. London. He hadn't exactly been sensitive then, had he?

Satisfied he was well-organised he donned his favourite cream fedora with the black band and picked up his briefcase. Today's assembly was about forgiveness. Not seven times must you forgive your friend, he would say, but seventy times seven, even if they've taken your best football cards. And who can tell me what seventy times seven makes? That's a great deal of forgiveness. His mental rehearsal was disturbed by the doorbell. Dominic liked doorbells. They heralded interruptions which fed his sense of self-importance. Whether it was a hesitant, single mother wanting a baptism and wondering about his response, the treasurer keen to go through the accounts, or a man of the road down on his luck and hoping for a bowl of soup and some cash, they would all receive the same friendly welcome. He would handle this caller as though he had all the time in the world, despite the inconvenience, and still be in time for assembly.

'Good morning, Sir. Revd Lane, is it? Dominic Lane?'

'Father Dominic Lane, to be precise,' said Dominic with the smile he usually reserved for young children. 'Or Canon Lane if you prefer. How can I help?'

'My name's D.I. Buckley and this is my colleague, D.S. Stephens. All right if we come in, sir, rather than standing on the doorstep?'

They flashed their I.D cards but Dominic could not focus on the text. His hands became clammy. His heart pounded. His breakfast did somersaults. He tried to control the muscles in his face. Was it Dad? They wouldn't send a Detective Inspector to tell you your father had been taken ill. Could it be the theft of the brass lectern? He hoped not. They'd already spent the insurance money. It was unlikely but was the oppressive burden about to crush him for good? Was this the knock on the door he had dreaded for years? All the energy he had put into atoning for the past: had that been for nothing?

'Well, er, yes, of course, but I was leaving for school. Year five assembly. Forgiveness. I'm due in fifteen minutes. Could meet you back here in an hour?'

'Afraid year five will have to manage without you this morning, sir. They'll have to think about forgiveness another time. You can make a call. Say you've been unavoidably detained.'

They produced the search warrant and two more officers appeared from nowhere. The nightmare became a reality. They sat him down in the kitchen and told him he was under arrest. He would be taken to an undisclosed location in London and interviewed under caution. His bishop had been informed. No, he couldn't make any phone calls, not just yet. Later. They searched every room in the house, including the attic. They emptied drawers, took books off shelves, opened cupboards. They confiscated his passport, and personal and parish mobile phones. His computer. Asked him if he had anything else hidden away in the rectory or the church that he'd like to tell them about. Make no mistake, they warned, they would find it if it was there. In response, all he managed was 'There must be some mistake.'

Dominic felt sick. He had been well-behaved in this parish, hadn't touched a boy, always careful to have other adults present whenever they got close to him. Obeyed all the safeguarding rules. Looking didn't count, did it? Maybe he wouldn't want the police to scroll through his mobile phone, but they must know the kids on the videos earned real money for giving themselves a good time. He glanced up surreptitiously to the top bookshelf. There was the funeral director's plastic urn containing, ostensibly, the mortal remains of Edna Henderson, a name he'd stolen from a gravestone. Surely, they wouldn't stoop to opening it. To distract them, he asked about getting a lawyer and they said he would have legal representation at the station.

He'd never be able to look his dad in the eye again. He imagined his family when they found out what had happened, and the hell they'd go through. He was the criminal, but they'd be crucified too, hanging alongside him. When the officer said they were ready to go, leaving the search team to continue their work, he picked up his overcoat, slipped the dog collar out of his black, clergy shirt with the frayed neck, and turned off the oven.

Sitting in the back of the car, looking out of the window, avoiding the stony-faced officer beside him, Dominic relived his past. In the '90s, the Church was threatening to ruin everything. There were endless arguments about women priests and he was constantly worrying whether he'd have to leave the Church for good. He wasn't going to swear allegiance to a woman, a woman whose holy orders were anything but holy. Escape routes had been provided in the form of 'alternative episcopal oversight.' Another fudge, another compromise – what the Church did best. In the end, it had worked out all right. He and his friends inhabited their safe bubble and ignored the rest. As long as you weren't downright rude to a woman priest – or a woman *pretending* to be a priest because they were all imposters – you could rub along. Just like you could be a gay vicar as long as you didn't flaunt it or get caught in the act. He and his friends had met in carefully chosen pubs after Evensong. Gone to discreet venues. It had all been going so well.

There were three teenage acolytes, all poised to carry the candle for the faith, literally and metaphorically, and all under age. Three fledglings; impressionable Christians ripe for the taking. That's what he'd thought then, the kind of language he'd used. Made him cringe with shame to think of it now. When he could stand it no longer, he'd found another job miles away, leaving his victims and his guilt behind. For more than twenty years he had got away with it. He'd hoped against hope those teenage boys would never breathe a word. They would be too afraid, humiliated, and embarrassed. That's what he'd relied on and he'd been right. Anyway, nobody listened to teenagers in those days. But the boys had grown into men.

He'd been terrified for a few months when Jimmy Savile had been splashed over every screen and newspaper. Even the Church had sat up and taken notice, but the danger passed. Inquiries, policies and grand statements materialised but nothing impinged on him directly. This was different, though. He was in the back of a police car speeding towards a moment of reckoning.

He could guess what had happened. A couple of months ago, Geoff's dad rang to congratulate him on being made an honorary canon of the cathedral. It was like getting a gold Blue Peter badge for long service and good behaviour. He'd even called him 'our beloved Father Dominic.'

'Saw it in the parish mag,' he'd said. 'Read it out over Sunday lunch. Not before time, Father, and richly deserved. Everybody was over the moon – well, nearly everybody. Geoff would have been, I'm sure, but he was a bit below par and had to rush out before he was sick all over the roast lamb.'

Geoff didn't have a bug. He would have been off to ring Sam and Sam would have rung Oliver and they would have gone blubbing to the police. And here was Dominic now accompanied by a duty lawyer and three police officers in a non-descript interview room in a grey police station somewhere in London. The lawyer's advice was clear. 'Admit to nothing, give no names or contacts, make no comment. It was twenty years ago and it's your word against theirs.'

Dominic followed the advice. 'No comment. No comment. No comment.' As he spoke the words again and again, he yearned to finish it and to shout from the rooftops. 'Yes, I did it. I did it. I'm guilty. Guilty as sin.' But he didn't say that because the lawyer told him not to, and because it was obvious what would happen to him if he did. His ministry would be over, his priesthood would be meaningless and there would be no way back. Ever. He knew what they did to people like him in prison, especially to hypocrites who hid behind the trappings of dog collars and vestments. If he made it out alive, he'd be pushing seventy. He'd never step inside a church again without signing a carefully worded agreement. He'd never baptize a baby or bury the dead. Parents would keep their children away from him, colleagues would look askance with contempt and pity and God would cast him into outer darkness. Ironic, he thought. He'd pronounced absolution and God's forgiveness on countless sinners and rogues but for this, he could never forgive himself.

They let him out shortly after midnight in a strange suburb with no phone and no cash. He still had his credit card. Across the road was a shabby motel lit by garish neon. Grey net curtains hung across the door and moved in the breeze. It was the kind of anonymous place he needed. He disturbed the night attendant, a woman whose hair was held back tightly in a scrunchy, wearing a sweatshirt that hadn't seen the inside of a washing machine for weeks. He was hardly in a position to insist on Egyptian cotton sheets or complain about the instant coffee, but she could have made an effort.

'Anything else for you?' she smirked as she handed him the entry card for the room.

'No. Thank you.' Thank goodness he wasn't still wearing his collar.

He pulled the door shut. The room was barely adequate but he didn't care. He was grateful to be away from the oppressive, grey interview room. He slumped on the bed with his head in his hands and rolled under the duvet. Tears streamed down his face. His head was spinning, the police officers' words ringing in his ears together with the echo of his own voice 'No comment. No comment. No comment.' He felt as if he'd been awake all night, but he woke before dawn. He washed, picked up his wallet, and asked the girl in the grubby sweatshirt the way to the nearest train station. He worked out how many changes it would take to get him home and drew cash from a machine in the wall.

By lunchtime, he was in Bishop Anthony's palace sitting on a plush sofa in his study. The police had advised the bishop days ago that the arrest was imminent and sworn him to confidentiality. He was not unkind, but there was no easy way to tell a priest he was suspended from all duties on full pay and should not contact his parishioners or the press. A recently retired clergyman, Brian, whose job was to be a friendly, listening ear would make contact soon. The bishop could not, he explained, given the circumstances, exercise such pastoral care himself. Dominic remembered how the bishop had gone on about his lengthy, faithful service when he'd installed him as canon. He, too, had called him 'beloved.' Words that sounded hollow and fatuous now.

Dominic went through the motions. He knew the score, knew the outcome, and knew the bishop had no choice. He neither confirmed nor denied what had happened, thanked the bishop for his time, and went home as if anaesthetised, driving like a learner for fear of causing an accident. Word would go around like blood seeping out of a body. He could guess what people would say as they sat in the snug at *The Dog and Duck* or waited at the school gate.

'Lock him up and throw away the key, the bastard.'

'Poor Father Dominic. What sick minds make such awful accusations?'

'If he's laid a finger on my grandchildren, I'll kill him myself.'

'When my old Mam was dying, he couldn't have been kinder. Father Dominic couldn't have done anything like that.'

'A man's innocent until proven guilty, but you have to wonder.'

Back at home, he wandered from room to room, picking up the things which made up his life, as though by touching them, he could commit them to memory before they were taken away. He sent an email to Roger, the churchwarden saying he would be leaving important papers – wedding applications, accounts, rotas, and an urgent hymn list for next Sunday – in a box on the rectory doorstep, and could he please collect them after dark but not call in because he wouldn't be available.

Roger would wonder if the allegations were true. Of course, he would, but he was discrete and non-judgemental. He wouldn't tell a soul, except maybe Harriet. By the time they beat their way in, it would all be over. He gathered up the washing, including the sheets from his bed, and left it piled up in the utility room. He cleared all the perishables from the fridge. An open packet of ham, half a quiche, a bowl of egg whites waiting to become meringues went into the bin. He washed everything up, leaving it to dry on the draining board. He took the casseroles out of the oven and dumped the contents at the end of the garden for the foxes. He worked his way through the pile of correspondence, filing much of it in the bin and adding a few papers to the warden's box. He wrote cheques to cover his bills, birthday cards for his twin nephews, and a letter to the agent in an attempt to cancel the Oberammergau bookings. He left the stamped envelopes on the hall table. Somebody would find them.

Every time the doorbell rang, he stood stock-still, until the caller gave up and went away. When the phone rang, he let the person speak before deciding whether to answer. He ignored them all except Brian, the poor sod designated to be kind to him, because he knew if he didn't, he'd be round to break the door down – in a caring kind of way. In a monosyllabic conversation lasting sixty seconds, he agreed Brian could drop in on Thursday. It made no difference to him.

Dominic spent his final hour gathering diaries, piles of old sermons from the days before he'd learned to work a computer, Lent course notes, anything representing his sham of a life as a priest. He piled it up outside the back door, made three trips with the old, wooden wheelbarrow and a final one with his laptop and the DVDs, CDs, and USB sticks which the police hadn't found. It had begun to drizzle and it was hard to see in the half-light. He struggled to push the barrow across the damp, uneven grass and half-tipped, half-threw the last load onto a bare patch of earth. He splashed a liberal dose of lawnmower fuel over the pile and struck a match, giving silent thanks for the seclusion of his garden. He grabbed a clawhammer, smashed the laptop and DVDs and added them to the fire. He watched until he was sure nothing was identifiable.

He had nothing to live for now. He went into the garage and stumbled over the tombola drum and the lawnmower. He picked up an old kitchen chair, took the tow rope from the boot of his car and went back into the garden, striding purposefully towards the oak tree.

2. Letter to Michael

Dear Michael,

Thanks for the latest card. I love Yorkshire and especially Wharfedale. I can't believe you stayed at the *Red Lion* in Burnsall just because I told you how Isaac and I spent so many afternoons playing around in the river there, rowing the dinghy, jumping from a rope tied to a branch. And fancy your visiting York University to see where I lived for three years. You even found Vanbrugh Hall. I'm impressed. You won't forget to tell me where you'll be next, will you?

When you promised to use Mum's pen to write to me, little did I think you'd be sending me such regular pictures of your travels around the country or that I'd be sending this missive to you from the confines of a retreat centre in the heart of Dorset. It was Roger, the churchwarden, who made it happen. Quiet, gentle, unassuming Roger. He spoke to the Archdeacon when he spotted what was going on. Didn't want me to burn my boats, or step over too many lines. I'd be out on my ear if it weren't for him. Not that having a breakdown is a capital offence but he could see I might say or do something outrageous and they'd lost one vicar in dire circumstances. I'm probably more popular with the bishop than Father Dominic, but only just, so it was just as well Roger stepped in.

The Archdeacon wasn't as prescriptive as Hamlet. He didn't quite say *get thee to a nunnery* but then I'm neither his mother nor his lover. He did, though, make me an offer I couldn't refuse. An all-expenses paid sabbatical in what amounts to a rest home for knackered clergy. He didn't use that word, either, but I knew that's what he meant.

That's why I'm here, learning what it means to be waited on, to be still, to sleep, and to eat food somebody else has cooked. And guess what? I don't feel one shred of guilt. In fact, I'm beginning to adapt to the lifestyle and thinking I might have a future. Some days, I wake up, listen to the birds, and am optimistic about the future. It's been a while since I could say that.

It may sound pathetic to go on about stress and burnout but people have no idea what it's like to be a vicar. How could they? They come to christenings and weddings and see us afterwards at the parties. They think we're the centre of attention and everybody loves us. And, of course, we only work on Sundays. Hah!

What they don't *see* are the emails, the texts, and the letters. Often, the content is untrue and some are downright offensive like the tweets you've probably read. Did you know the archbishop gets such libellous correspondence that his team don't show it all to him? And, like the archbishop, vicars can't answer back. We have to be gracious and forgiving. Well, I got fed up with that after a while. If you'd heard parishioners arguing about whose turn it was to read at the carol service, or why *she* always gets to do the Easter flowers, or if you've experienced the keening of grief when it is raw in the early hours of the morning, you'd know what I meant.

Nor do they experience the interrupted meals and the conversations which begin, 'Sorry it's dinner time, your day off, a bit late but . . .' Then there's the safeguarding nightmare, the policy documents, the pretence that you love the bishop's new project, plan, target or mission strategy, none of which has a grasp on reality. And the constant mantra about the importance of *growing* the Church. As if we weren't trying.

I sound jaded and cynical, don't I, and I'm only a few years in. I'm gradually remembering all the wonderful things – why I took the job at St Jude's in the first place, sharing people's most exciting and poignant family events. Even dying has its own beauty and there's nothing like the dawn service on Easter Sunday or the sound of children singing Away in a Manger at the Crib Service.

Anyway, it wasn't the hard work or the arguments and long hours which led me here. It was the tragedies, the heartbreak, the crap people suffer. The awful sadness, grief, and injustice. It's all the stuff that goes on behind closed doors that vicars get to share even when they'd rather not. It's knowing that, nine times out of ten nothing I can say or do will make any difference. And it became increasingly difficult to persuade people God was there, standing in solidarity with them. I began to doubt that myself and I hated having to pretend.

Now I've had a whole month to think, I can see that there were other factors. It wasn't parish life which finished me off. The real killer was my identity crisis; and my crisis of faith. It was cunning, creeping up stealthily and undermining me. All the time I was sifting through the detail of other people's lives, and being held up as a paragon of perfection, I was putting on an act. Not deliberately. Not at first, but deception is an easy skill to learn. It worms its way in until the charade even convinces you. Then I met you at Mum's funeral and something inside clicked. You were the catalyst so when I get tired of blaming myself, I'll blame you instead!

When I told the chaplain here that I'd read English at York, I realized how much I resented the church for dragging me away from my romantic idea of locking myself away in a shepherd's hut, writing endless bestsellers. I could have been the next Kate Atkinson or Rose Tremain, and been interviewed by *The Guardian*. Instead, I was a failed vicar of a suburban parish who couldn't summon the energy to write the newsletter, let alone a masterpiece. That was when she suggested I might need a complete break from ministry. Take a whole year out, she said. Write for my life. Get it out of my system.

After all, she said, she was going on maternity leave soon but it wouldn't stop her from being a priest even if she was at home changing nappies and mixing feeds. You can still be a priest without being a vicar, she said. Of course, I can. For a while. Maybe for a whole year.

So, I started writing. Straight away. And now I can't stop. My own stories came first. Stories about my childhood. Then about things which had happened to others. About Alex and Mum. It was almost too painful. There were times when I could only write for half an hour before I was blubbering all over the keyboard, but she was right, the chaplain. It was cathartic. Seeing the words on the screen made me think I was giving the characters credence and value. They and their stories would never be forgotten, though I was a bit creative with the facts.

Then, out of the blue, Roger made contact again. They couldn't find cover for the chaplain's maternity leave. He'd pulled a few strings, come up with a plan, and persuaded the other trustees I had made enough progress to be useful. I only had to say yes. If I would conduct morning and evening services during the week, preside at Communion on Sundays and be kind to the other guests, they would give me bed and board and a tiny honorarium.

'That's impossible,' I said to him as I sat on the bed, clutching the phone to my ear, paralysed with fear. 'What about St Jude's? A couple of months off is one thing but a year?'

'All dealt with,' he said, in a tone that allowed for no response. 'A vicar in the next deanery has to leave her parish in a hurry. Not her fault but the team rector . . . just don't ask. She needs an interim post for nine months, maybe a year. You'll be doing her and the archdeacon a favour.'

A thousand thoughts were rushing around my head. What about Alex, what about money, what if the new vicar changed everything, what if she was too popular and the congregation didn't want me back? After all, St Jude was the patron saint of lost causes and maybe I was just living up to the name. But even then, I knew I wasn't entirely lost. The idea took seed and now it's a reality.

Anyway, Michael, I didn't intend this to be such a long letter but there was a lot to tell you and it all happened very quickly. I become the chaplain at the end of the month and I can't wait to get going. I can banish the guilt about not working and I'll still have time for myself to write. I'm using my experience of sharing the lives of so many wonderful people, their living and dying, their struggle to let go as a jumping-off point. They won't be factual, word-for-word accounts, but the deep truth of every encounter will be there. Of course, I'll change all the names apart from my own stories, and maybe Roger and Harriet's. Nobody will ever read them, anyway. Only you and Alex. No self-respecting publisher would bother, even if I did pluck up the courage to send them off.

The first story is self-indulgent. It's about my 'formative faith experiences.' The therapist said it might help me to work out who I am, and why I fell to pieces. Just as our early experiences of loss, she said, affect how we manage adult grief, so our childhood picture of God influences our adult belief. I don't know whether she's right or not but I've taken her at her word. You're not obliged to read it.

One more thing. You said you were having tests. How, when, why? Don't die on me, Michael, not now. I'm not letting you go. Not now I know who you are.

Bethan.

3. The Red Skipping Rope

The counsellor I met at the Retreat Centre kept on about my 'current issues' stemming from my childhood. I thought that was true for everybody and so blindingly obvious it wasn't worth saying but I went along with her advice to write it all down, however passé it sounded.

I am five years old. Three days into my first term and I am shaking with fear. David Stone has commandeered the Play House for his H.Q. and Laurence Wilkinson the old oak tree with the hollowed-out base. They are the alpha males of the Infant School. The girls are the camp followers and the boys the foot soldiers. The diversity and inclusion officer has not yet been invented, let alone appointed. Everybody has to choose a gang to join and, as it's not clear who will be the winner, it's a difficult decision. I am scared of both of them. David has a military-style crewcut and Laurence has gangly arms and big fists but making no choice means a life of isolation. Making *any* choice is bound to lead to pain and suffering which no infant teacher or dinner lady (as we so quaintly called them then) can ever put right.

'I can't go back to school tomorrow, Mum. I don't want to be in a gang.'

'You have to go,' says Mum. Can she not hear the fear in my voice? 'You ignore the big boys and make other friends. When it's home time, we'll go and buy that red skipping rope we saw in the corner shop window.'

A skipping rope? Does she *really* think that a skipping rope, even a red one, is adequate compensation for confronting two six-year-old generals? We compromise. The next day, we will go to school just in time for the bell so that I can avoid the playground and creep into line. Being late terrifies me, and Mum, too, so we dawdle a bit as we get to the gate and then, giving her a quick kiss and wiping my eyes on the back of my hand, I race into the playground and line up. Kenneth Whitmore, the gentle, red-headed little boy with freckles and spindly legs is beside me in the boys' queue. 'I'm joining David Stone,' he whispers. 'Will you come with me?'

My school is a place of safety and learning according to Mum and Dad. To me, it's a place of confusion, endless pitfalls and traps. It's my first introduction to life away from the warmth of home, and from my cousins who live next door. The playgroup run by kind, middle-aged women in the church hall bears no resemblance to the noise and terror of a proper school classroom. The fifteen or so children I have shared toys with have given way to sixty infants in two Reception classes. On the one hand, excitement and promise are offered. I devour the reading books. Billy Blue Hat and Roger Red Hat live in *the village with three corners* and have exciting adventures involving ponies, sunshine and duck ponds. I gravitate towards the Play House (except when David Stone is in it). I love the smell of the hall's polished parquet floor and the tiny stiletto heel dents. I am attracted by the primary colours of the tryptich which hangs at a great height above the stage and tells me that God loves me.

We sing the same words every day: *God whose name is love, little ones are we, listen to the songs that we sing to thee. Help us to be good, always kind and true, in the games we play or the work we do.*

And yet, despite the avowed love of God, and my love for the *One, Two, Three and Away* reading scheme, Mrs Peel terrifies her desperate charges in the neighbouring classroom. Thankfully, my teacher is Mrs Gane but the fear seeps through the thin, plasterboard walls. Mrs Peel is overweight, has scruffy hair and wears shapeless skirts and polyester blouses. If she could, she'd be smacking the naughty boys every day but they've stopped all that now. It doesn't make her any less scary.

This is a place where we are made to eat lumpy custard including the skin, and soggy greens with meat pie whose pastry is thicker than the table. At least we don't have to drink lukewarm milk anymore because Mrs Thatcher has stopped all that though we can have it for lunch if we like. I never do because it makes me sick but, perversely, I yearn to be the monitor who skewers the silver tops and sticks the straws through the ragged holes. One red letter day, I am summoned for this important task. I am overwhelmed with pride and responsibility. Moments like these compensate, but only just, for the snares set to trip me up.

We are into our second term when Mrs Gane announces that we are going to make a card for Kenneth Whitmore. Kenneth is off school with a bad cold so I assume that's why, though nobody sent me a card when I had tonsillitis. Kenneth and his family are going to live in Torquay. He will be leaving at the end of next week. Mrs Gane smiles as she says it as though this is a piece of routine news. Torquay? Where on earth is that? Why can't he still come to school? We moved from an old bungalow to our new semi-detached house but we still have to go to school. Who will hold my hand when David and Laurence gather their armies at either end of the grassy play area? My fears tumble out on the walk home.

'Kenneth's Dad has a new job,' says Mum. She knew? And didn't tell me. 'Anyway, you've lots of other friends now. Maybe you could write to each other.'

I love him, I want to yell. He's my best friend. I need him. Kenneth comes back to school for his final week. He is distraught. He writes his new address on a piece of drawing paper from the wet-play box and I write mine in a notebook that I give him as a leaving present. It has a dolphin on the front and costs me half of my week's pocket money. He promises to write every week and to come back in the summer. Now I have the whole Easter holidays to worry about returning to school without him.

Without my best buddy, I am even more terrified of putting a foot wrong. I dread seeing a critical, red pen mark in my News book so, I write the same thing every morning. *We had eggs and bacon for breakfast. We had eggs and bacon for dinner. We had eggs and bacon for tea.* I have double-checked all these words in my dictionary. Mrs Gane tells Mum that, although I lack imagination, I am bright enough to go to Girton. I don't want to go to Girton, wherever that is. I want to go to Torquay.

Mum thinks I will be distracted by joining the Brownies. They wear uniforms and their sleeves are covered with badges so I leap over the toadstool and promise to serve God and the Queen. I wonder what the Queen will need from me but she only has to say the word. I will also swear undying loyalty to God if Kenneth comes home from Torquay, and Mrs Peel stops shouting. After all, his name is Love and I thought I was one of the little ones he was meant to protect. At the Brownie church parade, I am anxious again. Am I one of the *miserable offenders*? Where are the cheerful ones hiding? And what will happen to the slow people if we only believe in the quick and the dead?

Writing this all down, reliving those early days, makes it come to life again. I tell myself that Mrs Pugh will be long since gone but my stomach still churns. She can't hurt me now. Kenneth Whitmore probably forgot me as soon as he was settled in his new school and discovered that he could play on the beach every day. I expect his Mum bought him a new, red bucket and spade. He could be in prison now or in Australia, on his third wife. Maybe the sweet, freckled ginger-haired boy turned into a vandal. Let him go, I tell myself. Let them all go.

I am eleven years old now and in my first year at Grammar School. My friends and I are covertly watching two first-year tutors as they walk off the stage after assembly one Monday morning. Miss Finch teaches biology and Mr Webster history. Our antennae are attuned to spot any sign of romance – a stolen glance, a private smile. We've seen them together in the greengrocer's buying potatoes and cabbage so we suspect they may be having an affair, but this morning they hang around at the back of the hall waiting for us.

Miss Moss, the draconian deputy Head says the first years must stay behind. Panic sets in as we size each other up warily. What unknown line have we crossed, what minor regulation have we breached? Not wearing a beret or cap on the way to school is almost a capital offence. Miss Moss beams at us but it's not a smile an eleven-year-old can trust.

'We have a special visitor today,' she says, 'and he has brought a present for you all.' We breathe again. Things are getting better. 'First, he will talk about his work as a member of Gideons International.' The man is wearing a grey suit and a grey, knitted tie. A grey raincoat hangs over the back of the chair and a grey, checked pork pie hat sits on the seat. He looks like a spiv. I don't know what they are but it's a word Dad used about Uncle Fred and he had a hat like that. He reminds me of the Kleen-eze man who calls once a month with a carload of oven gloves, tea towels and lemon squeezers but there is one important difference. The Kleen-eze man is always cheerful.

Several cardboard boxes are piled up at the side of the stage and Miss Moss is poised, scissors in hand. The man tells us how Gideons International started in the United States of America and then came to England in 1908. All the members are married men and most of them are commercial travellers – salesmen who distribute bibles alongside their everyday wares. Bibles? Our present is a bible? That's no better than a red skipping rope. At least you could play with that.

Men like him, he says, leave copies of the New Testament and Psalms in hotel rooms, prisons and residential homes and give them to new pupils in secondary schools. Men like him are *advocates for the lost*, (who sound a lot like *miserable offenders*) he says and dedicate their lives, presumably when they are not selling stockings or bed linen, to *telling people about Jesus*. The Bible will help us when we are in need, he says, and be our friend and *an everlasting source of hope*. We can find recommended sections for when we are desperate, anxious or uncertain. Does he know something we don't? Perhaps I will find that elusive verse to help me survive double physics and double maths on the same day. It's not a great advertising campaign. No catchy slogan like 'Things go better with Coke' or 'Have a break, have a KitKat' but, thankfully, we'll have somewhere to look when we are suicidal.

Miss Moss summons Miss Finch and Mr Webster to unload the boxes and distribute the small, maroon books and, while this is happening, we may ask questions. Lily Ellis asks why they are called Gideons and the man explains that God gave the name to one of the founding members in a vision. Gideon is in the book of Judges, he says. It's a great story involving a fleece and a battle against the Midianites. Lily Ellis, who has been given her bible, says she can't find the book of Judges anywhere and the man's cheeks redden. 'That's because it's in the Old Testament, dear.' Miss Moss glares. Lily is wise enough not to ask the next, obvious question.

I toss up in my mind whether to speak and decide it's worth the risk. After all, time spent in the hall is time stolen from double physics. 'What if a man doesn't have a wife?' I ask. 'Can he be a Gideon?' The man puffs up proudly. 'No,' he says. 'This is an organisation for husbands. Men who have wives.'

I keep my hand up, avoiding Miss Moss's gaze. 'And what about the wives? Do they take bibles and give them to people?' He snorts with laughter. 'No, dear. Of course, they don't. They are at home caring for the home and their children. They support their husbands so that the men can do the important work.'

It's not much of an answer and not much of a present but it has kept the watts and volts at bay. Miss Moss, who has neither a husband nor children of her own, jumps in, makes a brief speech of thanks and we all clap half-heartedly.

My second brush with what I now know to be evangelism occurs two or three years later. Ann Oxford University Mission is coming to our town and a host of events have been arranged. The town centre church, St Martin's, resembles a fire station but has stunning modern stained glass through which the sun floods the interior. A simple, tall cross hangs on the wall behind the altar. *Youth* are invited to come to special services and it will be fun says the posters that have line drawings of smiling teenagers in jeans and trainers. There will be orange squash and cake. No expense has been spared to save the younger generation from the fires of hell.

Despite my dis-ease about the grey, Gideon man and his sexist answers, I have found myself reading the little book every night in bed and am keen to learn more so I dip in and out of the Oxford Mission bible studies, discussion groups and slide shows. When I turn up, early, for the finale, I am met in the foyer by John, an undergraduate demi-god. He is broad-shouldered and tall and has wavy, black hair. He is reading divinity at Oxford and is an enthusiastic convert. He offers me a service sheet as if he has been waiting for me alone. 'Have you given your heart to Jesus,' he asks, smiling like a vicar. What I want to say is 'No, but *you* can have it any day.' Instead, I mutter something vague and non-committal and brush my long, blonde hair out of my eyes in what I hope is an alluring way. Is loving the messenger as valid as loving the Lord? Not a question I dare ask him and, of course, I never see him again. Anyway, he wouldn't have been a patch on Kenneth Whitmore.

More concerning than the demise of my first love and the disappearance of my Oxford idol is the demise of the God I was persuaded to believe in. Something clicks inside my head. I've spent all my adult life thinking that God's name was Love, that he would listen to our songs and prayers and, provided we were *good, always kind and true* we would be rewarded not just in heaven but on earth forever and ever Amen. I've been fooled into thinking that the ancient texts of scripture had an answer for everything if only I searched hard enough.

I've been believing in the wrong kind of God. For forty years. I've been deceived, living under an illusion even Paul Daniels couldn't have conjured up. I didn't know who my real father was and I didn't know who my heavenly Father was – and I didn't know that I didn't know until it was almost too late!

If God was Love, his Church would reflect that love. It would rate women alongside men, alleviate grief and suffering and it certainly wouldn't have let Father Dominic loose on an unsuspecting world.

4. The Parish Profile

When a parish advertises for a new vicar, they produce a Parish Profile. It's a hybrid document, influenced by several voices, and resembles an estate agent's brochure. They don't tell downright lies but present facts that show things in the best light.

I sat at the kitchen table scrubbing away at the red ring left by last night's bottle of Malbec. My vicar, Gavin, had come for a breakfast meeting and was brushing toast crumbs onto the floor. Together we were scanning the ads at the back of the *Church Times*. Three months before my curacy came to an illustrious end. Three months to find a job. In equal measure, I was excited and terrified by the prospect of independence, but what if I made the wrong decision and fell into a snake pit? I'd been hoping for a sign from heaven. One of my more earnest colleagues had told me I would get a shiver down my spine or a tingle in my arm, a sure sign of the Holy Spirit, but thus far, no joy. God had been silent.

'It's a buyer's market,' said Gavin. 'Loads of jobs out there especially if you're prepared to go north and don't have unreasonable expectations.'

'Bishop of Winchester's not a viable option, then?'

'Maybe next time.'

'Anyway, I hate purple.'

'I suggest you avoid these dioceses,' he said, rattling off three or four areas where the bishops' views on women and gay people were suspect. He pointed to a green and purple icon at the top of an ad. 'This one says he is fully supportive of women, but he isn't, not when push comes to shove; and this one will only appoint evangelical clergy. Straight ones.'

'What happened to *wise discernment and prayer, competence and calling, spiritual sensitivity*' I asked. 'What about this bit here, the bit that says *Every decision will be surrounded by prayer, every interview held within the love of God?*'

'Yeah. Right. Remind me how long you've been a member of the Church of England. We all start out looking for a glimpse of God's wisdom when we make decisions, even bishops, but like it or not, politics gets in the way. Does your face fit, did you train in the right place, are you willing to play their games without always knowing the rules?'

After Gavin had gone, I sank into my favourite basket chair, turned the music up, and smiled at the photo on the coffee table of me and Isaac standing with Mum. She'd be so proud of me when I became a proper vicar. I worked through the eight sides of adverts again, striking out a few with a red felt tip, and circling others in green. It was depressing. I didn't want to be a "Pioneer Leader of a Lighthouse Hub" or a "Facilitative Mission Enabler", or in charge of thirteen parishes and sixteen church buildings. In my wildest dreams I couldn't imagine running a parish with a population of twenty thousand, with or without a team, and some of the language used made me suspicious. What exactly was a "fresh expression community doing contextual ministry in an inner-city environment"?

I wanted to be a vicar, plain and simple, nothing more, nothing less. I wanted a church called St Mary's, St Paul's or St Peter's, with a tower or spire, and a hall with stackable chairs, and green cups and saucers. I wanted to minister to rich and poor people, young and old, the good, the bad, and the ugly, to share their deepest joys and sorrows and, with a following wind, to help them stumble towards God. Perhaps I was a dinosaur and that wasn't what people wanted but it was what the bishop had called me to do and all I had to offer. God was a God of love who loved his little ones. My task was to share the workload.

My mobile quacked. Gavin's call sign. He'd only left ten minutes earlier.

'Had a call from an old friend. Archdeacon of Five Bridges. Interesting vacancy, but they don't want too much publicity. Asking for recommendations from people like me.'

'Inside job? Old boy network? Chat behind the bike sheds and all done and dusted. Everything I've always complained about.'

'More like avoidance of embarrassment. Keeping the press at bay. Protecting the Church's reputation, respecting the dead. I'm sending you the draft parish profile but keep it to yourself for now.'

I googled the diocese, the parish, and the village, and read the profile. I knew that it told me more about the compilers and less about the reality but I devoured it anyway, trying hard to read between the lines. They were giving nothing away about the history or reason for the secrecy. I read on.

"Swannery was originally a hamlet. It is now a large village and fast becoming a small town. The improved transport systems and the growth of the commercial and light industrial parks have led to the population rising consistently, but it remains an ordinary, workaday place where families thrive, older people are cared for and children are nurtured and valued. There is an army camp outside the village and we have several shops, a community centre, office blocks, a museum, a post office, and a bank, not counting the food bank. A two-form entry primary school, with Cygnets nursery attached (children, not plants!), a comprehensive school, and a girls' private school fulfil all our children's educational needs."

The attempt at humour was a little grating and the signs of over-hurried writing annoyed me but left me itching to find out more. My eyes glazed over at the pages of statistics and accounts but I knew enough about money to think up some intelligent questions if I made it to an interview.

"Bishop's House is a popular nursing home and several small businesses have made their home with us. The old railway station is a café and the goods yard has been turned into a playground with carefully designed climbing frames, swings, and balance bars. There are two ponds opposite the playground and a bigger one hidden behind the trees on the edge of the village where geese and ducks can be seen in abundance."

There were photos, too. It looked and sounded too good to be true. A proper church with a spire and a hall where Brownies and Cubs meet and the sun always shines. A surgery, a dentist, three charity shops, an optician, a branch of the C.A.B., and a pub called *The Dog and Duck* where they *serve luxury fish pie in individual dishes, tapas, and burgers on slates*." I couldn't imagine using the tattoo parlour, and I'd give the nail bar a miss. I hate food on slates so I might have to find a different local. Mentally, I was moving in.

The profile made no attempt to disguise the tensions between Upper and Lower Swannery, but I noted the church and vicarage stood right in the middle on the unmarked border between the two. A sign of hope, maybe. The previous incumbent had *excelled at holding the communities together*. Why had he left, then? Everybody was remarkably quiet on that front. The website was veiled in euphemisms and I stopped myself from searching press releases. Maybe, in this case, ignorance was bliss. For now, anyway.

The next day, the archdeacon rang me. He said the community was still shell-shocked, six months on. Father Dominic, much loved for twenty years, had taken his own life. At the time the press had taken up residence on the village green, giving attention not even Magda relished. Many mixed emotions were at play: disbelief, anger, and grief all rolled into one. 'Right up your street, he said, 'according to Gavin.'

It was also a place, he said, where single parents did three jobs and were reliant on the food bank and benefits, while others were cash-rich and time-poor. But they all went through the same life experiences: anxiety, love, stress, death, disappointment. Money didn't inoculate anybody. I was about to say I'd worked that out for myself long ago but thought better of it.

The upshot was that he asked me to complete an application form. The interview process would be less formal than usual. I would meet the Wardens first and then, if we were all keen, a small group would be invited to a social gathering. Just to be double sure.

'I'll send the form to you today,' I said, opening my laptop again.

5. Pimm's in the Garden

Part of the 'discernment' process is a social gathering fondly known as 'trial by quiche.' My 'trial' was more niche than quiche and after I'd met the Wardens was an opportunity for others to size me up.

'It's like this,' said Magda, a churchwarden who had lived in or around Swannery for forty years. 'It's like we have several worlds in our village. The world you see when you walk down the street, the faces exuding respectability, the caring fathers and loving mothers showing a picture of contentment. And the world you don't see.' I had barely opened my mouth to respond when Magda launched into her next topic.

'Children are going to school without any breakfast. Can you believe that, Bethan? The fact the foodbank can't keep up with the demand says it all.' She offered the plate of chocolate eclairs around and took another one herself.

'Have you read *Under Milkwood*? Dylan Thomas? Swannery has its version of Myfanwy Price, Captain Cat, and Rosie Probert although it's nowhere near Wales. I expect you're wondering how I'm so knowledgeable. I've been a councillor and a counsellor so I've seen and heard everything in one capacity or another.'

I wondered how anybody got a word in edgeways when Magda was in full flight. On the other hand, she'd get things done and was a useful source of information. She was a big-boned woman, with a mass of black, natural-looking hair, and an aquiline nose. She dwarfed the other warden, Roger Parmenter, who sat holding his coffee, biding his time, watchful.

'And you, Roger' I asked. 'What do you do?'

'Roger is a very important lawyer,' said Magda.

'A lawyer, yes,' he said. 'Retired. Not an important one. Do you have any questions for us, Bethan?'

A few days after the pseudo-interview, the Archdeacon rang. The Wardens wanted to offer me the job as long as I survived quiche and Pimm's in Roger's garden. Father Dominic had been dead for six months he reminded me and the wardens were desperate to move things on quickly.

'Sorry,' he laughed. 'That isn't meant to be as insulting as it sounds. I don't mean they'll take anybody with half a brain. You did well at the interview. Roger was especially keen.'

I wasn't surprised that Magda hadn't been as sold on me as her colleague. He said she supported the appointment but thought I was inexperienced, a bit naïve, too *unusual*. She can talk, I wanted to say. That was the problem. She could talk – for England. She should have given me a chance to answer her questions, instead of answering them for me. She went on and on about the psalms holding the solution to all life's problems and, according to her, she knew everything about the people of Swannery. Power-crazed. Bossy. Officious. Full of herself. All of the above, but nothing I couldn't handle.

The half a dozen people who had come to give me the once-over had drifted off. I wasn't sure if that was a good or bad sign. Roger, who'd been very quiet at the interview, came into his own now we were on his home territory. He and Harriet were spoiling me with proper Pimms, not the Aldi imitation I was used to. He intimated that the job was mine if I wanted it, and the bishop would write to me formally.

'I'm not going to tell you all about the past,' he said, as we sat in the sun. 'It's the future that counts now.'

I didn't want to contradict him, not this early on in our relationship, but in my experience, you can't escape the past. It's there whether you acknowledge it or not. Anyway, I was sure I'd be given several accounts of Father Dominic's life story, his good and bad points before long.

'What about the future, then,' I said. 'What kind of vicar are you hoping for? Not counting prayerful, spiritual, and almost perfect.'

Roger laughed. 'Should we assume you're not the archangel Gabriel?'

I looked straight at him, trying not to smirk.

'Thank goodness for that! What we need is a leader to pull together all the . . . er . . . groups within the church.'

'You were going to say factions, weren't you?'

'The vacancy period . . . we don't call it an inter-regnum here in case vicars think they're royalty . . . has been interesting, challenging, jolly hard work and a breath of fresh air.'

'Tell me about the fresh air bits.'

'Father Dominic was – traditional. In every way. Despite what happened, he remains a blessed memory for many people, but he took his status and authority very seriously.'

'At least you all knew where you stood.'

'Yes. Indeed. But once he was gone, unexpected people stepped up to the plate, one or two rather too enthusiastically. Those who liked being told what to do were all out of kilter, and others sensed freedom and went off ploughing their own furrows. Lots of good things happened. Our bereavement group took off, Little Fishes has doubled in size and a pastoral team has been going into Cygnets and the primary school.'

'You're not hoping for somebody who can do everything single-handed, then; a kind of omnipotent saviour?'

'I think that post has already been filled, hasn't it? But we are hoping for a mediator. A team-player. A person, a woman, who can listen to all sides, bring people together and unite us.'

'Assuming that particular woman isn't the cause of other arguments,' I said. 'I'm guessing not everybody will be as delighted by my appointment.'

'Don't mind Magda,' he said. 'There's more to her than meets the eye. She'll come round, and she's very influential. Get her on your side as soon as you can. Of course, it would help if you had a jolly husband and two children – preferably one of each.'

I liked Roger's humour. We would get along fine. 'There's KitKat,' I said, tongue in cheek. 'My cat.'

Roger coughed. Sipped his Pimm's. Looked into the distance.

'There are two main challenges. Sadly, Father Dominic's death split the community down the middle. A few have left the church for good, taking their money with them. For the first time ever, we're running a deficit budget. And secondly, we've become too inward-looking. We're irrelevant to whole swathes of the parish, especially the poorer end, and it's as though the wider world doesn't exist.'

I observed the carefully tended gardens, the ornamental

pond with its Italianate fountain, and the apple trees standing in the far corner. Picked up the blue-tinted glass and sipped my drink.

'That's enough to be going on with. I'm exhausted just thinking about it all.'

'Tell me more about yourself,' said Roger, handing me the remaining home-baked cheese straws.

'It was all on the application form. I have a cat called KitKat and a brother, Isaac. There's not much else to say.'

Not exactly the truth but I wasn't ready to share anything else. Not yet. Not even with Roger.

'You've broken all the records.' Gavin could barely conceal his pride. 'Ten days from the first phone call to getting an appointment letter from the bishop. Wish all my curates found it that easy to get a job.'

'And now an interminable wait for safeguarding checks,' I said. 'Let's crack open a bottle and celebrate before I die of excitement or change my mind.'

6. The Poppies

Alex was different from anybody I had met. I knew a lot about gay people, less about trans people and nothing about inter-sex people. I do now.

I first spoke to Alex on the eighth of November. I know I'm right about the date because it was the night before our Remembrance Day services. We were scuttling about like worker ants. The stewards were tidying flyers and programmes left behind by schoolchildren, squaring them up in neat piles. The organist was fiddling around on the keyboard, discussing musical options with her deputy, and a band of women were touching up the poppy display which ran down from the pulpit like the river flowing through the town centre.

Father Dominic had filched the idea from the Tower of London and the church had been doing it ever since. We couldn't match 888,000 ceramic flowers on stalks but we'd done our best. The Tuesday Group had met at the library every week and knitted and crocheted like there was no tomorrow. Then they'd spent hours fixing the crimson works of art, mostly recognisable as flowers, onto strings and wires. The effect was stunning. Even the belligerent rebels, the ones who said we were encouraging nationalism and glorifying violence, had made admiring noises.

Magda, Fiona and Audrey had been in charge of the whole venture, though Audrey had dropped out halfway through, seeming to lose interest. They were flower arrangers and sopranos in the choir, and one of the choirmen had nicknamed them the MAFIA. It made me chuckle in private but it was a grossly exaggerated slur. They were assertive and a bit scary, but nobody could deny that their hearts were in the right place and they got things done. I often wondered about their individual stories and what they would tell me.

Magda was smiling. 'It's quite attractive,' she conceded. 'Don't stand too close. With your red hair, you might be mistaken for a giant poppy.' A rare instance of an attempt at humour. I was winning her round.

Alex had been in and out on a few occasions. More out than in, but that's not unusual. People are drawn into the building, but think one step past the font will lead to an irrevocable commitment. They take offence if nobody talks to them but panic when they do. They worry their whole soul will be laid open to public scrutiny or that you will ask them whether they love Jesus. This time, she wasn't going to get away without a conversation, however minimal.

'Afternoon,' I said. Surely nobody could resent such an innocent opener. 'I'm Bethan. You've been in before, haven't you?'

She hesitated. Her mousy hair framed a long, thin face. The fringe covered more of her eyes than was helpful and it was clear she hadn't broken the bank when she chose her clothes. Not exactly scruffy, not down at heel but ordinary and shapeless, as though she had no interest in her appearance. The purple and silver brooch provided the only hint of colour. Was it an orchid?

'I'm Alex. I've come because it's the day of remembrance.'

Not one for chit-chat, then.

'Well, strictly speaking, not until the eleventh but it's the civic service tomorrow and we've had children in every day. Nothing like a poppy and a bugle to attract the crowds.'

'No. Not *Remembrance* Day. It's the Intersex Day of Remembrance. Eighth of November.'

I swallowed. Coughed. Tried to hide my confusion. Did I miss that module at theological college?

'Ah,' I said, playing for time. 'And that has special significance for you?'

She pushed her fringe back with one hand, showing nails bitten down to the quick. Then she looked me straight in the eye.

'Yes. It does. There's a good reason my name's Alex. It meant they wouldn't have to change my name whatever they decided to do about me.'

I pretended to be distracted by the sound coming from the organ pipes to disguise my embarrassment and hide my curiosity. I thought I'd heard everything. Obviously not.

'That's what they did back then to people like me. Plumped for one or the other and got on with it.'

'This is worth more than a chat at the back of the church on a winter's afternoon, isn't it? Fancy a coffee? Talk more?' Alex nodded and exhaled as if she had been building up to this moment for a while. I had been assessed and had passed the initial test.

We met a week later at Alex's favourite coffee shop opposite Superdrug's fire escape at the end of a narrow *cul de sac* off the High Street. It was run by a couple of Italian guys. It had concealed corners and alcoves, and the smell of the freshly ground coffee beans and almond croissants was seductive. A glazed, ceramic pot filled with trendy uneven brown sugar lumps sat on every table, and the November Specials menu was rolled up in a tiny, milk bottle. We ordered a Latte, a double expresso and two croissants. Nobody hugs like an Italian and Luigi and Gino greeted Alex like a long-lost sister. Luigi pulled a chair out for me and rested his hand on my shoulder.

'You be careful now,' he joked. 'People might get the wrong idea.'

I wasn't sure what to think about our conversation. It wasn't counselling but more than a chat; not straightforward pastoral care. More like a mutual exchange of sensitive information. We just talked. Well, she did the talking and I listened and asked questions. I learned what the Intersex Day of Remembrance was and what the World Health Organisation's views were, but who cared what the WHO thought or what the International Commissioner for Human Rights had to say? That was all second-hand and theoretical. Alex lived with the reality every day. She was the one who mattered, the person sitting beside me with her orchid brooch and scruffy hair, and all the others like her, forced to live covertly beneath clouds of embarrassment, discomfort, and shame.

Alex had finally worked out why she was different after she'd managed to extract her medical records from her G.P. She'd been in her early twenties by then and had a couple of health scares. The G.P., close to retiring, had been reluctant, although he knew she had a right to see her notes. Was Alex sure she wanted to read them? Damn right, she did. She'd taken them to her attic bedroom, locked the door and read every note. What they'd done to a helpless, three-year-old disgusted her.

'I considered slitting my wrists,' she said. 'I researched everything on the net, how to do it, what to use. I wanted to make my dad suffer. Feel guilty. But then I realized I'd be another statistic in a random medical journal. What good would that do?'

Instead, she confronted her father.

'We did what the doctor thought was best,' he said from behind the sports pages. 'We went along with everything. And we didn't tell a soul, because he said it would be worse for you.' He refused to say any more. Her mum may have been more forthcoming, more repentant, but she'd died before they'd been able to have a conversation. Alex blamed her as much for that as for what she'd allowed to be done to her daughter. I felt sick. My stomach churned in the old familiar way, but Alex didn't appear to notice.

'I don't know if I'll ever forgive them for what they did to me. Dad is still convinced they did the right thing. He said Mum didn't want people to laugh at me at school if I went in the wrong toilets.'

'You can see their point.'

'When I'm rational, I can. I believe their intentions were good. They were trying to be kind and it was a horrible decision to have to make. But then I get angry about not having had a choice and something mega happening to me and never being told.'

She wasn't the only one, I thought, who might make that complaint against their parents.

7. The Doll's House

Father Dominic had taken the funeral of Daisy and Eliza's Mum and I was approached to 'sort out' the ashes. It didn't take exceptional sensitivity to spot the tension between the sisters but months passed before I was privy to the whole story. It was ages before I realized Daisy was married to Titus whose father, William, was connected to Eliza, and that Titus and Daisy's daughters played with Eloise. That's why it's a minefield being a vicar in a village. You're never quite sure about the connections.

'You never know, we might find a rare Clarice Cliff pot,' said Rachel. It would be cause for another argument if they did.

'Unlikely,' said Daisy. 'It's more like that ridiculous programme where they auction off a garage full of junk to the highest bidder. Except you'd have to be brain-dead to bid for this lot. You can *see* what rubbish it is.'

Barely a month after the funeral, the sisters have spent the morning in the attic, throwing away half-eaten cardboard boxes and plastic sacks, investigating packages that haven't been opened for decades. 1960s Christmas decorations, old clothes and the hand-written teacher training essays, worksheets, and handouts, long since out of date, carefully filed away in labelled box files. Father Dominic, the vicar who took the funeral had made a thing of Mum's love for children and all she'd done for the primary school in her day. He'd been kind and understanding. Who would have thought . . . but it was only gossip, though you had to wonder. Now they'd have to negotiate with the new vicar about scattering the ashes. They should have done it months ago but they've both been pre-occupied and hadn't agreed on what to do with them.

'Penny for them,' says Daisy. 'Come on, still plenty to do.'

The boxes and bags are lifted out, manoeuvred down the stairs, and stacked in the hall. The four-by-four is loaded.

'Finally, the monster vehicle comes into its own,' says Rachel. There was plenty of room for it on the drive of Daisy's brand-new five-bedroom house on the most desirable estate in Swannery. She considers Titus her brother-in-law's salary obscene and rarely misses an opportunity to register her disapproval.

Shall I go through this lot at home?' asks Daisy, flicking through the insurance documents, pensions and bank statements. 'They go back to the year dot. I'll be better at identifying what's important.'

Thirty-fifteen! thinks Rachel, as the barb of criticism sinks in.

'OK. I'll do the charity shop run. I don't expect you have any idea where it is, do you?'

'Or maybe take it all to the tip and be done with it,' says Daisy.

They exchange a grudging kiss. Daisy zips up her Rohan Kendal jacket with its two-layer Barricade Standard insulation and leaves for the school run. Back in the house, Rachel eats a cut-price sandwich and then mounts the loft ladder. She peers along the rafters, checking for safe places to stand. She glimpses it, peeping from behind the water tank. Her doll's house. She had no idea her parents had kept it, especially after everything that had happened.

She steps tentatively across the beams. There have been enough accidents. Just touching the house brings a lump to her throat, and on a depressing winter's afternoon, as she perches in the dusty loft surrounded by mouse droppings and a lifetime's garbage, Rachel begins to cry. Her shoulders shake, and the tears flow. Even grown women have their limits, she thinks and, no, Daisy, I can't pull myself together. Their father fell off a ladder and died three years ago; their mother went to bed one Sunday night and never woke up; three rounds of invasive IVF have produced nothing but disappointment, and she will find out in two days whether the last little embryo has made it. Her husband prefers to be on the oil rig than with her and to top it all, she has been thrown together with Daisy to salvage what is left of their childhood. Surely, she has a right to be upset.

She is transported back to her childhood as she touches the wooden roof. She is jumping up and down unable to contain her excitement. Mummy has told her she can choose the wallpaper for the spare room. A new baby sister is coming.

'But it might be a brother,' says the precocious four-year-old. 'And why aren't you as fat as Jeanette's mummy?'

They explain that Daisy has already been born but her mummy and daddy can't look after her. They have chosen her to be their second little girl. Rachel is ecstatic. She'll be one up on everybody at school, having an adopted sister. Her teacher will have to pay attention at circle time. She, singlehandedly, will save this baby from monsters and dragons like the heroes in her storybooks. She will be the fairy godmother and the baby will love her and be grateful. And she, Rachel, the *real* daughter, will still be her parents' favourite.

When she comes home from school the next day, she is surprised to find, not a baby swaddled in a blanket, but a child wedged into an armchair, sitting up by herself. She has curly hair and four teeth.

'Where's the baby,' says Rachel. 'You said we were getting a baby. A baby would be lying down.'

Beside the chair is a bulky parcel with RACHEL written on it.

'Daisy isn't a brand-new baby,' says Mum. 'She has been living with her foster carers for a while. She brought this present for you because she loves you.'

Rachel is well aware no child can go shopping by herself, and how can Daisy love someone she's never met, but she keeps quiet. If Mum wants her to believe that, she'll play along. She doesn't want to risk losing the present.

Wiping her eyes on her sleeve, Rachel struggles to shift the doll's house from behind the chimney breast. She eases it through the hatch and, slowly, brings it down onto the landing. The house is hers and she is reclaiming it. No sharing with Daisy. No wheeler-dealing or compromise here. It is smaller than she remembers. The familiar green, metal windows hang precariously on their tiny hinges. The plastic 'glass' is yellow and cracked but the red-brick paper, faded and ripped in places, is not beyond repair. She can hear the matchstick gate creak and smell the cotton wool woodsmoke swirling up the chimney pots.

Pictures of herself and her dad in a railway model shop choosing trees and shrubs for the painted plywood garden flash, uninvited, into her mind. She tentatively prises the front open. The nursery is pastel pink, a replica of the real one, and has a tiny basket chair and a shocking pink carpet. It must have been her pink phase. The balsa wood crib has a white, lacy quilt that is suspiciously like a snippet of net curtain. When she recognises the guest room where Grandma used to sleep, warmth floods through her veins. A tiny knitting bag lies under the chair and a dressing gown hangs on the door. Gran was often with them in those days, helping Mum and keeping the peace when things went wrong.

'She was my grandma *first*,' Rachel would yell at Daisy. 'And it's *my* doll's house; not yours. You don't belong here. Tell her, Grandma.'

In another bedroom is a miniature straw girl wearing pigtails, a pinafore dress and a red school jumper. The wallpaper has miniature, hand-painted flowers on it. Instantly, she realises the care her parents had taken and how careless she had been with their efforts and their feelings. She would have done anything to stop Daisy from joining in.

The promised baby, who was supposed to lie quietly in her crib, was beginning to crawl. She demanded attention and snatched Rachel's toys. Daisy was not the slightest bit grateful to her for saving her life and, against all the wisdom in the books which the precocious Rachel took from her mother's bedside table, Daisy did not behave like a troubled, adopted child. To cap it all, the sister whom Rachel had expected to overshadow in every way, turned out to be a gifted musician.

'Why can't I have a violin?' asked Rachel petulantly.

'Because you wanted to play the flute.'

'We're all different,' Dad had said. 'Daisy's musical. You're good at other things.'

The plywood lawn has dirty green shrubs, and splodges of orange paint represent her childish attempt at flowers. The paddling pool's water is scrunched up tin foil. She begins to shiver. Her heart races, her head spins and she hides her face with her hands, hoping the memories will fade. In her mind's eye, she can see the two of them in the garden on a blazing summer's afternoon. She can hear the splashing and screaming, adult voices yelling over one another as they rush into the garden. She feels their strength as they pull her away and plonk her under the cherry tree, shouting at her to sit down and stay still or else. Dad is thumping Daisy on the back and she is coughing and spluttering all over the lawn. It is as vivid as it was then – the day she nearly drowned her sister. Now, here she is aged thirty-five, motherless, childless, with a failing marriage and a sister who barely tolerates her.

Daisy and Titus may be annoyingly rich and speak with pretentious accents but they are the only relatives she has apart from Steve and she's lost him to the oil rig. She can't blame her seven-year-old self for her jealousy, but the adult Rachel should know better. Is there time to make amends? What if she tried to see things from Daisy's perspective? At the funeral, Father Dominic had suggested they all 'take a moment and forgive one another, let go of the past.' The words of the invitation had stayed with her, skulking under the radar.

'This can't go on,' thinks Rachel. 'What have I done? One of us could die like Mum and Dad and it'd be too late.'

She picks up her mobile. 'Daisy. It's me. I know it's late and you're busy with bath time and stories but can I come over? Now. No, it can't wait. No, I haven't found a Lowry. But I *have* found my doll's house. Dad made it for me and

I wondered whether maybe Mia and Sophie would like it and. . .perhaps they'll be better at sharing than I was.'

8. The Librarian and the Car Salesman

Philip Larkin got it right. He would have been extremely rich if he'd had a tenner for every time somebody quoted him. Parents don't intend to fuck you up; it's not deliberate or vindictive. They can't help it, and blaming them for everything isn't right. I heard about Gillian on the grapevine. Keith lived out of town but you couldn't get arrested on suspicion of murdering your mother without word getting around.

Gillian Small was thirty-nine years old and had never been kissed. Not in the sexy, passionate way she dreamt about; not in the rough, erotic way she read about in the popular romances she was ashamed to admit she smuggled out of the library in her tote bag. True, there had been childish fumbling and hand-holding in the Play House with Hugo Markham but Hugo had kissed every girl in 1A and half the girls in 1B. She wasn't special; never had been. And who was to blame? Her bloody parents. That's who.

She had never forgiven them for ruining her teenage years. The time when normal kids were allowed to push the boundaries a bit and work out who they were, they had stifled her, embarrassed her, and discouraged her from doing anything remotely daring. For them, taking a risk was trying a new washing powder. Other girls in the sixth form went to Marbella to celebrate finishing exams. Gillian spent the week at a caravan site near Cromer. 'Foreign boys are after one thing, darling,' said her mum, which was exactly why Gillian wanted to go. While her friends were experimenting with sparkly eye shadow,

Gillian was helping her mother to make a rug. While they were devouring *Smash Hits*, Gillian was listening to concerts recorded from an ancient thing called the Light Programme, while her dad sang along to Mantovani. She would kill Mantovani if he weren't already dead.

The thing was, she'd never wanted to use Romantic Ruby lipstick. She'd only stolen one from the pharmacy for a dare to prove she wasn't a complete wimp. She didn't want to scream at long-haired boys alongside dozens of hormone-driven teenagers and she didn't want to drink illicit pints at *The Dog and Duck* but that wasn't the point. You had to pretend you did if you wanted to have any friends. Instead, she had waved the others off to university where they inhabited pods, shared clothes and ran up debts. She stayed at home in the 1930s semi with its Artex ceilings and 1970s wallpaper. Bit by bit, her parents had suffocated her with their petty attitudes and smothered every good idea or ambition she ever had.

She started her first job at Swannery Library. The building was old and outdated with its red-brick walls and high windows, its poky rooms, and gloomy corridors. It had a distinctive library smell. Not musty, but leathery and papery. More like the odour of well-behaved students and elderly literati. They promised to refurbish it to make room for the IT suite and the community hub, but it was a Grade II listed building and the rules and regulations were complicated. Of course, there was no funding. There never was.

All she had now were shelves of books of murder mysteries and her imagination. She'd read everything starring Miss Marple and Hercules Poirot but, in their stories, the unpopular uncle or miserable professor was dead within the first few chapters, leaving only the thrill of the chase to amuse her. So, she graduated to thrillers where you heard the screams, saw the instruments of violence, and imagined yourself there, wielding the baseball bat or kitchen knife. There was no harm in it, she told herself.

She had met Keith at St Jude's Book Club. Last week, he had given her a present and almost kissed her.

'But it's not my birthday.'

'Does it have to be? This is just because . . .' He'd leaned in and she'd held her breath, but bossy Magda had breezed through the door with a plate of flapjacks and ruined the moment. Gillian was disappointed when she opened the box of three, white handkerchiefs, and more disappointed when she saw the Oxfam sticker. But they were brand new, and she forgave him when she saw the letter G embroidered in each corner. How thoughtful he was; just not practised in giving voice to the romantic feelings which bubbled inside him. Not yet. But she would change him.

Keith was a bachelor and a few years older than her. He had been living with his mother until her death three months earlier. Slowly and surely, he said, he had put his head above the parapet. Joining the Book Club was one way to meet people, he said. Kind, safe people who wouldn't judge him. Gillian loved how he always wore a tie and brown brogues. She wanted to iron his shirts and run her fingers through his fine, ginger-tinged hair and do other, unmentionable things to him.

He was an accounts manager for a hire car company, he said. In the back room, juggling figures, moving numbers from one spreadsheet to another. She had no idea how anybody could do that all day, but being a librarian wasn't big on excitement either. It was hardly the most scintillating conversation starter. The dramas in her life were found between the front and back covers. Nothing exciting ever happened in the flesh.

Life was full of opportunities now, said Keith, because he'd inherited his mother's house and a rather healthy bank balance. For the first time in his life, he was truly free. Was it possible to be truly free, she thought? Even if you were thirty-nine and had never been kissed?

Gillian came home from the Book Club on Tuesday night flushed and jumpy. She chatted away as she boiled the milk for the cocoa, and gave her mother a peck on the cheek and her father a quick squeeze on the arm. Whatever happens and wherever she ends up, that chocolatey smell will stay with her forever.

'Night, Mum, Night, Dad. Thanks for everything.'

Dad raised his eyebrows at Mum, who shrugged her shoulders.

'Night, night, sleep tight. Don't let the bed-bugs bite.'

Same old, same old, thought Gillian. One day, I will kill them. Safe in her bedroom snuggled in her knee-length, winceyette nightie, she drafted a letter. It was now or never. The ticking of her biological clock had rarely troubled her but now its alarm was ringing with regular monotony. She wasn't sure whether she wanted to be a mother, but she sure as hell wanted the right to make that decision for herself. What she did want was fun and riotous sex and adventure and she wasn't going to get it making the cocoa. If she didn't do something dramatic soon, her life would be over before it had begun.

She paused for inspiration and pulled down the pristine suitcase. She chose and discarded, folded and packed. She wouldn't need many things. Keith would buy anything she wanted. A few favourite books, her wash bag, a purple make-up bag with its pristine contents and the red shoes. She'd bought them in a fit of pique but hadn't dared to wear them. She hesitated over the photo of Mum and Dad outside the caravan, fought the temptation to smash the glass, and stuffed it in the inside pocket. She packed the embroidered handkerchiefs carefully and zipped the case shut. Gillian finished the letter, folded the unscented Basildon Bond writing paper, and sealed the envelope. It was brief and to the point. Silly to get all emotional at this stage in the game.

She sat upstairs at the front on the early morning bus. Too early for schoolchildren or shoppers; only a few night shift workers on their way home from the supermarket and grey women with raincoats who looked like they'd fallen on hard times. The streets were dark and it was drizzling but it didn't matter. Today was the first day of her new, real life. True, a tiny part of her felt guilty. Mum would be up soon making the tea while Dad snuffled away under the duvet. She would see the blue envelope by the kettle and open it with the silver knife she kept on the hall table. She would read it, adjust her glasses, rub her eyes and re-read it before letting out a whimper. Then she'd walk upstairs, clutching the letter with one hand and the bannisters with the other, stopping at the top to catch her breath.

'Dad. Oh, Dad.'

Sitting on the bed beside him, she would read aloud. 'I have gone to be with Keith. Will be in touch.' Mum would go into overdrive, giving voice to the unquenchable, internal martyr who was always ready with a complaint or opinion. How could she do this to us, she would say. After all we've done for her. I gave up my career. Chose not to have more children. She never lacked anything and now . . . The sentences might come in a different order but this is what she would say. Gillian had heard it all before. Her dad would swivel around in the bed, put on his slippers and dressing gown, tie the cord and go to the bathroom with the avocado basin and worn-out lino before he uttered a word.

Gillian was five minutes away from Keith's. She took deep breaths, hardly able to believe this was happening. She had done it: left home, made a stand, broken out. She was free for the first time in thirty-nine years. No more boiling milk to make the fucking cocoa. Her stop. She walked down the stairs holding the handrail, picked up her case from the luggage rack, and stepped down as though she regularly travelled on a bus through a suburban residential estate at six-fifteen in the morning.

She knew her way from here, even though it was her first visit. Keith wanted to decorate it all before inviting her to what he hoped would be her new home, he'd said. Up the road, second on the left and first right into a *cul de sac*. The bungalow was at the end and had a low box hedge and a magnolia tree in the front garden. Keith had told her about his hard work, pruning the tree to let more light into the living room. Daylight was gradually breaking through the clouds. If this were a story, there'd be a rainbow any minute now.

As she rounded the corner, she stopped. There was a police car outside the house which she was sure was Keith's. Had she confused left and right? Dad was always saying she had no spatial awareness. Or maybe the policeman was a mate who'd popped in for a bacon butty. At six forty-five? You'd have to be pretty friendly to do that and she didn't think Keith had many mates.

She walked down the path and glimpsed a black uniform through the window. Unsure whether to turn back or forge on, she reminded herself her new life was about to begin and she had done nothing wrong. Not yet. She saw Keith sitting on the sofa, shaking his head and heard his raised voice. Saw a second policeman with a mug in his hands, bending down towards Keith.

'Can I help you?' said the officer as he stood, legs apart, purposely blocking the doorway.

'Keith. What's happening? Are you all right?'

'Gillian? What on earth are you doing here?'

'And you are?'

'If it's any of your business, my name is Gillian Small and I'm a friend.'

'I'm afraid it's not convenient now, Madam.' He was about nineteen. Who did he think he was?

Friday morning at nine 'o'clock. She was sitting on a bench in the corridor of a utilitarian police station several miles away from home. She had no idea why they had to bring him this far. It had taken her two bus rides and a short walk to get there. She was wearing the red shoes and new make-up, an Oxfam handkerchief slipped into her pocket.

She had called in sick on Wednesday and had spent the last two nights at Keith's poking around, opening drawers, checking out his dead mother's jewellery, flicking through files and folders. The wallpaper in the main bedroom would have to go; along with most of the furniture. The curtains wouldn't survive a hot wash which was just as well as their days were numbered.

She sat in the garden with her morning coffee, admiring the shrubs and trees with their berries and leaves, wondering which she would transplant and which she would dispatch to the compost heap.

They will let her see Keith, they've said. They will release him once the bail conditions are sorted. She must be patient. She'd waited nearly forty years so another hour or so wasn't a problem. She has to stop herself from gasping when she is shown into the interview room. He is half the man he was in the Book Club. Unshaven, no tie, ashen-faced. Is this a man she can love and cherish? Probably not but he has money now, and a house, so she must think carefully before she abandons him.

'Why are you here?' he asks. 'What's going on?'

'I'm a good friend,' she says. 'The kind of friend you need.'

'They're letting me go. Section 114 of some Act or another says it's OK if they don't think I'm a threat to anyone else.'

'How could you be?' she whispers.

'They think I murdered Ma,' he says, with an expression that dares her to side with them. 'I gave up everything for her. Cared for her to the bitter end but the coroner isn't satisfied.'

They sit in awkward silence. She's bored with listening to people feeling sorry for themselves. She's thirty-nine and has never been kissed. Not properly.

'Will you come home with me?' he asks.

She hesitates for a second too long. 'Of course,' she says. 'Why wouldn't I?' Her mind is working overtime. She must keep her cool, pretend to be excited as though she is still in thrall to him. She wants to wipe the lipstick off with the Oxfam handkerchief and throw it in the bin but she must bide her time. If they don't get married, she won't get the house and the money when Keith, wracked with guilt and grief, meets a sticky end. She will play the long game.

'I can't wait for us to get home,' she says. 'At last, we'll both be free. And together. But tell me . . .' she leans into him, mouths the words. 'How did you do it?'

9. Father's Day

Loneliness is a terrible affliction. All the friends in the world can't compensate for that one special person. People are living longer, sometimes with great joy but sometimes with frustration, pain and isolation. Vicars are privileged to contribute to difficult conversations about dying and living.

'For God's sake, Pa,' said Titus. 'This is absolutely not going to happen. There is no way on earth I will let you go through with this. How do you think it will go down in chambers? I'm a criminal barrister in case you've forgotten. I can picture the headlines. *City lawyer helps father take his own life*, or in the tabloids, *General Belvoir murdered by barrister son*. Do you want to ruin my career? Just because Esther Rantzen's been making noises, doesn't mean you have to follow suit.'

Faye, his sister, wriggled, shuffled a pile of magazines and rearranged them neatly on the table beside her.

'There's no point in arguing, Titus. My mind is made up. If you and Faye won't help me, I'll have to go sooner rather than later. Alone.'

The grandfather clock ticked, marking the silence.

'Do you have any idea what this will do to me, Pa?'

'It's not all about you, Titus,' said Faye. 'It's about Dad and what he wants. It's his life and his death.'

William studied Faye's face. Registered the shock on his son's face. Titus had always got what he wanted. Every achievement, and there were many, was celebrated. His opinions were imbued with divine authority. Living in Belvoir House surrounded by his ancestors' portraits had given him a false impression of his importance. Faye had never made the same mistake. Had never entertained inflated ideas of her status. Rank counted for nothing if you were faced with a succession of crippling death duties and no means of paying them. Social standing counted for nothing if you were self-centred and unpleasant.

It wasn't Titus' fault. She blamed her parents for giving him a ridiculous name encouraging him to be pretentious. Ellen had said he must have a giant's name to be a giant in the world; a name people would remember.

'It was such a difficult birth,' said William, knowing he had told the story many times before. 'Ellen nearly died. You were such a tiny scrap. You were more like a Timothy than a Titus but I couldn't deny her anything.'

'And I was baptised Titus Harold Belvoir,' said Titus, like a child reciting his times' tables 'and to hell with what anybody else thought.'

'Yes,' said William.

'But we're not talking about Titus, Dad. We're talking about you. It's the present and the future we should be considering. Not the past.'

'I have thought of nothing else but the future for the last six months,' said William. 'I've lain awake at night, alone in my bed, thinking about what will happen at the end, what a burden I shall be to everybody, and how undignified it will be.'

He removed his glasses and polished them slowly on the embroidered napkin he retrieved from underneath the cushion. The matching chair sat opposite him, silent and empty.

'I do still have all my faculties, as you can see. I've done my research, spoken to medics, revised my will, considered the current law, and read every conceivable document on the website.'

Titus leaned forward and opened his mouth to speak but William was ahead of him.

'I know the course this disease will take. It's not a decision one makes on a whim.'

'You've left nothing to chance, Dad. You must have been planning for ages,' said Faye.

'You're tackling it like a military campaign,' said Titus. 'But even a General has to listen to his fellow officers.'

'And then, when he has listened, he makes his own decision,' said William, and then, under his breath. 'And that's what I'm going to do.'

All the private agonising, all the pros and cons of every option, all the statistics he had gathered poured out in a rush.

'And I'm not expecting you will take my side, Faye. You're not a child anymore. You don't have to oppose Titus for old times' sake.'

Titus and Ellen supported Oxford in the Boat Race. Faye and her father cheered for Cambridge. They loved the theatre so Faye and he became film buffs. There was no animosity, no harm meant. It was the way the family worked and played, but dying wasn't a game.

He watched Faye's eyes move to the dozens of photographs on the window ledge, the same ones that used to sit on top of the baby grand in the drawing room. Titus, holding school trophies, Titus, throwing a mortarboard in the air, Titus, doing anything. Titus and Ellen were always close enough to be touching, his head leaning against her, her arm slung casually around his shoulder. Faye's school photos were hidden at the back. William castigated himself again for not noticing that Faye appeared less significant in every sense. If Titus was a warship, she was a dinghy seeking shelter in a protective harbour. It would have been so easy to redress the balance.

'I'm sure Faye will decide for herself,' said Titus, 'but what about her career? What do you think the management at Bishop's Place will have to say?' He spoke quietly and rationally now, squinting at Faye out of the corner of his eye.

'It's a Christian foundation for a start. Do you think families will want her ministering to the needs of their geriatric relatives when they hear she's been an accomplice to your suicide? That's what this is when all's said and done. They'll say she helped you on your way.'

The heat rose up William's cheeks, the muscles at the corners of his mouth tightened. He gripped the arms of his chair and leant forward.

'Such emotive language is beneath you, Titus. You're a barrister. Assisted dying is not illegal in Switzerland or Holland or Germany as you well know, and there is precedent for family members accompanying their relatives and not being prosecuted. I'm not asking either of you to be with me, necessarily, but to support me when I decide the time has come.'

'It's not that easy, Pa. Not since Shipman. People are ultra-sensitive, and with good reason.'

'But that's for me to worry about and deal with,' said Faye. When had she acquired this new confidence? 'You're well aware well the drugs are self-administered. I don't agree with Dad's decision, either, should you be the slightest bit interested.'

'You don't?' William's voice faltered. 'Neither of you will help me?' He'd expected resistance from Titus, but Faye? She'd never let him down before.

'I didn't say that, Dad. I think you're wrong but it's not me who has the disease, and not for me to judge. If it's what you want, I'll support you in any way I can, including getting on a plane and pushing the wheelchair.'

William slumped down with a deep sigh. Titus groaned.

'It would be a bit odd, wouldn't it,' said Faye, 'helping other people's relatives to make independent decisions and then trying to control my own flesh and blood when it matters most. I'm not sure what the Foundation will think. I'll work that out when the time comes.'

It was the boldest speech Faye had ever made.

'Why. . .why do you think I'm wrong?' His confidence was ebbing away. 'Which bit of the truth have I missed? Has there been a medical breakthrough that will stop me from being unable to move, speak, control my bowels or swallow? Where is the new wonder drug which will make my final weeks and days bearable?' Tears were forming in the corners of his eyes. Titus appeared to be struggling for words. That would never have happened before Ellen's death.

'Not a medical miracle, Dad, nor a wonder drug. Not yet at any rate. I'm not saying it will be a picnic. You will lose your independence but most people do, however peacefully they die. I want you to talk it through a bit more, meet my colleagues. Online research and pamphlets don't tell the whole story.'

William watched as she reached across to adjust the faded curtains to protect him from the glare of the afternoon sun. It gave him time to think. Maybe he was wrong. Could he have a few more years left before he lost his dignity? Faye was offering a different approach, seeing things from another angle. She worked with the elderly and the dying every day. He should listen to her. Perhaps he was being a little short-sighted, a little hasty.

'There's a man in one of our apartments who thought he had a few months to live and that was three years ago. He still drives his Mini Cooper, visits friends, and, last month, he went to his grandson's passing-out parade at Sandhurst. If he'd booked a one-way trip in desperation, he'd have missed it. Anyway, medical research is always developing.'

'Except Brexit has seen off loads of research scientists,' said Titus, 'and the funding has dried up.'

'Shut up, Titus. Why don't you go and make the tea? I'll come and get the cake.'

Faye reappeared from the kitchen with a chocolate cake, three plates and linen napkins. Titus followed closely behind with a tray and the best tea service.

'Mustn't forget it's Father's Day, Pa. May there be many more to come.' He rummaged in the sideboard drawer for the silver cake knife. This domesticated version of his son was a novelty William was beginning to enjoy. Faye snatched the knife and began to cut the cake.

'This would have been different if Mum had still been here, Dad, wouldn't it?' she said.

'Yes. Mama would have talked sense into you,' said Titus with half a smile. 'You wouldn't be thinking like this. She wouldn't have let you.'

'She isn't here, is she? That's the trouble. That's why I need to take things into my own hands and get it over with. I can't go through this without her. I just can't.' His shoulders heaved, and he sobbed, then slumped in his armchair in a room that, like him, was looking very tired.

'Dad, I'm wondering whether this is more about grieving for Mum than being scared of dying. Your career has taken you to pretty dark places and you've seen some awful things.' She stirred the tea, sniffed the milk, poured it into cups, laid a warning hand on Titus' arm. William wiped his eyes with a grubby handkerchief. He blew his nose and ran his fingers through his hair.

'I. . .I. . . maybe it's. . .I should have been driving her into town. It should have been me, not her. But she was in a hurry, and I wanted to finish balancing our accounts and she said she could manage, she'd post the Christmas parcels, go to the library and pick up prawns for lunch. When she was late back, I assumed she'd popped round to yours, and then there was somebody knocking at the door, and after the police had gone, all I could think of was whether the prawns were going off and what we would have for lunch.'

'Dad. It's all right to cry. You can't be brave all the time. People often say and think strange things when they get terrible news. And if you'd been with her, it wouldn't have changed the outcome.'

'Father Dominic said all that, too. He was such a lovely man. But it might have done; changed the outcome. I'd have been driving and either I'd have avoided the motorbike, or I'd have been in the line of fire and not her. I can still smell the engine oil and picture it running all over the road. I'd give anything to change places with her.'

He saw Faye was crying.

'I can't look at a prawn now, let alone eat one. Turns my stomach. Takes me back to that Saturday morning. I wanted you to think I was fine and could cope. Didn't want to upset you or be a burden. It doesn't get any easier, however many months go by.'

'Oh, Pa. Why didn't you say anything? You seemed so … so in control, so together.'

William hesitated. He couldn't tell Titus that he had never been in control, that when he saw him touch the coffin as they followed it into the chapel, he was taken back thirty years to the day they had watched their eight-year-old son rushing back for one more hug as they left him standing on the prep school steps.

'I didn't want to ruin Christmas any more than it already had been. Then there was the funeral and you had the girls, Titus.''

'Here's a plan, Dad,' said Faye. William and Titus liked plans. 'Let's put this conversation on hold for a bit. How about Titus and I come and stay next weekend? Just the three of us. We'll go through all the albums, sort out Mum's jewellery and her tapestries. Do the things we should have done months ago. Let's get food delivered, no prawns, and be self-indulgent for the whole weekend.'

William sipped his tea. His eyes locked on the soft greens and blues of the Isle of Skye wall-hanging. He could picture Ellen sitting in the chair opposite him every afternoon, the teapot on the table, flapjacks, or whatever she'd baked that day, on her favourite plate. There was always a half-finished tapestry or a scrap of knitting stuffed down beside her cushion. He missed her more than he could say. He pretended he hadn't seen Faye kicking Titus' shin under the table.

'Yes. Good idea,' said Titus. 'I can rearrange the diary. Daisy will be fine with it if I'm home for Sunday bath time. Could be here by seven on Friday. Maybe bring a bottle or two to help things along.'

'Well, if you're sure. That would be, well, wonderful. It's her jewellery and the sewing things I couldn't face.'

'And then we can have another chat about the future and what you want to do with the rest of your life,' said Faye.

'But for now, Dad, Happy Father's Day.'

10. Tom's Story

If there was ever a challenge to faith, it's the unexplained or unexpected death of a child. Nothing compensates for that particular son or daughter, brother or sister. Where was the God whose name is Love when the chips were down?

'Where on earth have you been all summer, Tom?' says Cathy. 'Saw your kid sister outside the nail bar. She said you were away somewhere. Didn't sound convincing. You've been messaging weird stuff, too. Not still sore about me and Dinesh getting off at the ball, are you?'

I pause before answering. Absorb what, for Cathy, is a long speech. Take a deep breath. Close my eyes. I've missed them this summer, not that I'd tell them that in a million years. I've known most of them since the reception class at Swan Meadows. Only Becca is missing. She's given up 'A' levels and gone to do an NVQ in hairdressing. We've shared everything. Acne, detentions, boasting we'd be the first to do it. We've agreed to take over *The Dog and Duck* every time one of us turns eighteen. I'm the oldest, so it'll be my turn first. Lucky that, given the circumstances.

'Had brain surgery.'

Laughter breaks out on all sides. 'Yeah, right,' says Dan.

'Not funny, Tom,' says Cathy who is more sensitive than she lets on.

'It's true. Still sore, as it goes, but not like you mean.'

I display the bald patch at the back of my neck. It's not that big but it's like a crater to me. I can feel the draft and, when I style my hair, there's an annoying gap. I still have to put special cream on the scars so my fingers smell of antiseptic every time I touch my head.

'Spent a bit of time in hospital. Still seeing specialists. No big deal.'

Cathy, whose arms are entwined around Dinesh, pulls away from him. Gasps.

'Brain surgery? Tom? If this is a joke to make me feel guilty, then it's working. I thought those headaches you had were stress from . . . '

' . . . you dumping him?' says Dan.

The voices trip over each other, Babel-like. When, what happened, how, why didn't you tell us?

'Didn't have time to tell you,' I lie. 'It's a full-time occupation being a medical phenomenon. Don't need to talk about it. I'll keep you posted. Just don't try to be nice to me because I'll see through you.'

We are the new Year Thirteen, trying to grow into our roles as the most senior students at St Jude's Comprehensive. Mr Young, Marcus Young, the deputy head, has given us a pep talk and told us how we must be responsible, setting good examples for the students below us. We've all taken it seriously but not one of us would admit it. Doesn't do to be too keen.

'How about you lot? What's happened to you?' I ask. There's silence while they wonder what to say. I know what they're thinking. How can they top that? Anything they've done will seem lame and meaningless.

'Crewing on the yacht in the Bahamas,' says Cathy, eventually, 'with Mum and her new man. You can't imagine how blue the water was, and how warm. Wish I hadn't been, though. I'd have been here for you.' She means it, too. Normally, she'd be fiddling with her hair, and opening her eyes wide, playing for attention. Today, she sounds flat, not trying to impress.

'Finally finished my silver Duke of Edinburgh's ready for the UCAS application,' says Dinesh. He's the one with the over-enthusiastic work ethic and the demanding mother. Dinesh is mixed race, and his white, middle-class Mum worries employers will hold it against him. She's probably right especially if he hangs around in a monochrome place like this.

'Earning money,' groans Paddy. Paddy's family, fashionably described as *blended* by his social worker, is overflowing with love but light on cash. 'Mum's expecting again. Another boy. She's not best pleased.' For a split second, I hate his mother. I am my mother's only son. She'd do anything to keep me alive.

Some people go on expensive cruises, some work in supermarkets, and some get off with other people's girlfriends. And me? My summer's been different. I have a malignant brain tumour. Get over it. They say they can slow it down if I'm lucky, but they can't kill it for good. Today, I'm smiling. I've missed the goading and being told I'm a nerd. For the moment, things are all right. We're together again for our final, exciting school year if you can call 'A' levels, UCAS forms and interviews exciting. If it's going to be my last, I'll have to make the most of it.

There's no point deceiving myself. I'm not going to be an engineer. I wanted to be one before I could spell the word. In Cygnets, I made a castle from cereal packets, in the Juniors a balsa wood aircraft and a pinhole camera, and the canal boat lift I designed for my GCSE project won a prize. We tried it in the bath and it worked, for a few minutes, anyway. I had endless plans but there's a lump the size of a golf ball in my head. So, I have a choice. I either join in with everyone else, like I believe I might go to Uni, or I sit at home listening to podcasts or gaming while I wait to keel over. It's not much of an option, but I've decided to join in, pretending I'll still be around this time next year.

Upstairs in the staff room they'll be talking about me, though I can guarantee the headaches I give them won't be in the same league as mine. Mr Young will tell them they must treat me like any other student. Don't embarrass or make him feel awkward but don't ignore him either. And don't avoid the elephant in the room. It's O.K. to use the word cancer. In return, they'll try to project confidence they don't have. I know how they feel.

Mr Young's partner, Damian, is my maths teacher. We're allowed to call him by his first name now, he says. He thinks it will make us work harder if he treats us as equals. It doesn't make a blind bit of difference, except we're embarrassed and avoid calling him anything, but he means well. He'll ask me about the prognosis and whether I can keep up with the work. He knows I struggled last year, and it won't get any easier now, but it's not a problem, is it? I'm unlikely to see inside an exam hall again and even if I do, it won't matter if I fail.

The deputy head will be relaying Mum's message. The consultant says there's always hope, but it's a complex cancer. They should prepare for the worst though he won't talk about timescales. Mum won't have told them the whole truth, for sure. She's struggling to come to terms with it herself. I don't talk to her much, not about emotional stuff. I talk to Bethan, the new vicar. She's been in a few times and I like her. There's a bit of her that reminds me of myself. She doesn't pretend it's not happening or tell me Jesus loves me and that it will be lovely in heaven.

In July, OFSTED gave the school outstanding, and the exam results in August were the best for years. It's been all over the front page of the Recorder, and we're riding on a high. I've put a dampener on everything. I hope the teachers aren't as pole-axed as Mum and Dad were when we sat in the consultant's office. I'll never forget those words.

'Tom. Paul. Louise. It isn't good news.'

'Sorry, Mum,' I'd said when we saw the scans, and it was obvious that big boy wasn't going anywhere in a hurry.

For a moment, I felt guilty for not trying harder. Maybe I could have taken more care. Irrational, I know, but the mind plays tricks, especially when it's fighting an unwanted and destructive intruder.

'How you doing, Tom?' asks Damian, when we bump into each other on the stairs. I can see he's trying to hide his discomfort behind an over-enthusiastic greeting. It's tricky for him to get it right. If he shows no emotion, he could be accused of being heartless. If he overdoes it, we both look stupid.

'I'm here, as you can see. Don't go asking me how I'm feeling, O.K.?'

'It's a deal. Tell me if I can help or if you need extra time for assignments. I'll leave you to call the shots.'

I grin. 'I'll certainly need a few shots,' I say. I am grateful he is prepared to play it my way. He's not many years older than me and I'm not sure who needs more reassurance. I smile again. Funny how I'm turning into the protector when I'm the one with the brain tumour. It happens all the time.

Like Kate and Jo. I cried for them. I'm their big brother. Just not doing a very good job. Such a pain they are, most of the time, with their silly, girly friends and their make-up and nail varnish and skin treatments taking over the bathroom and yet. . .and yet I had to stop myself from hugging them and saying how upset I was I wouldn't be there to keep them safe.

A week might be a long time in politics, but six weeks is a hell of a time in the life of a sarcoma. At the ball, I had my whole life ahead of me, with or without Cathy. Life is short. Often too short and there's nothing you can do about it. Dad used to tell me to grab every opportunity with both hands, but it's too painful for him to say it now so I lecture myself instead. I'll never be a proper engineer. But if I can engineer ways of making the end easier for everybody else, I will.

I've talked to Bethan about my funeral. She'll be good at it. Calm, warm and honest, holding everybody else together. And then she'll fill her bath with bubbles and cry. That's what she told me, anyway. There will never be a summer like this one. There'll never be another summer of any kind. Not for me.

11. The Telephones

I used to think that DA (domestic abuse) was confined to the poor, the uneducated and readers of the Daily Mail; that it happened in shabby homes with untidy gardens where old washing machines sat on the front lawn. I had no idea it was as prevalent in the gated communities of large, impressive houses, amongst the rich and the famous. Perpetrators might be bankers, builders, teachers, politicians, window cleaners or clergy. You just never know!

She punched in the numbers under the glare of her ever-watchful husband.

'Heather? It's me. Afraid I can't make it tomorrow. No, I can't rearrange. Not sure where my diary is. Have to go.'

She replaced the phone carefully in its cradle *everything in its proper place* ringing in her ears.

'Good girl. Not difficult, is it?'

Henry Bull smiled as he stroked her cheek, causing her, as always, a deep sense of dis-ease.

'You don't want to go gadding off to London by yourself. You'd have to get a bus to the station, get the right train and then find your way around the underground. And do it all in reverse. You don't know the difference between the Jubilee Line and the Docklands Light Railway. You could get yourself into all manner of trouble. Anyway, who would get my dinner?'

'Yes, Henry. You're right. It was a silly idea. Only, I haven't seen Heather for months, and I don't think Mum is doing very well in the Home.'

'Heather's no good for you. She puts ideas into your head and winds you up. When you're with her you always spend money on things you don't need. Your mother is perfectly safe. She won't be missing you. Last time, she thought you were collecting for the Salvation Army.'

He laughed.

'I'm sorry I get over-emotional, but we don't know how long she'll be with us.'

'Good girl. Let's hear no more about it. I'm off to the Council meeting. Can't keep them waiting because I'm giving the presentation. Important business to conduct. Why don't you watch David Attenborough once you've cleaned the kitchen.' It was a command, not a suggestion. 'See you later.'

The door slammed. She loaded the dishwasher, wiped down the worktops with extra strong kitchen cleaner – *germs are deadly* – recorked the wine and prepared the cafetière for Henry's return. When she was sure she had left everything exactly as he liked it because he was always telling her how important it was not to make him stressed, she checked that three shirts were hanging in the wardrobe for him to choose from in the morning, hangers all facing the same way. She laid matching cufflinks on the dressing table and put a clean, ironed handkerchief beside them. She had never dared ask, but she'd often wondered whether Heather put her husband's clothes out every night.

Once upon a time, she would have had a sense of pride in the successful accomplishment of routine domestic chores but, nowadays, nothing she did satisfied her. She longed to ring Heather, but Henry had itemised bills and would check. She loved her sister and her mother. She needed to be sure Mum was well. There was still time before David

Attenborough would induct her into the fantastic world of gibbons. Did she have to watch it because Henry had said she must? She probably should. What else would she do otherwise? And Henry would quiz her on every last detail. He said it was because he was interested in helping her learn, *widening her horizons* but occasionally she wondered if that were true.

She gazed at the telephone table. The anniversary of her father's death was fast approaching. He'd died decades ago, but she could still remember standing in the school hall for assembly and reading the school motto engraved on the headmaster's pulpit. AMOR OMNIA VINCIT. *Love conquers all.* 'That's a lie,' she'd wanted to shout. 'We loved our dad, but that wasn't enough to conquer anything.' She had loved Henry, too, the best way she knew, but he was the one who always did the conquering and she was always the victim.

Where was the phone anyway? She was sure she'd replaced it. She knew she had. Hadn't she? Panic struck. What if she'd thrown it away by mistake? Henry was right. She was stupid. That's why she didn't have a mobile in case she lost it. It would be such a worry, Henry said. If it was stolen, anything might happen. Thieves were so clever nowadays. Heather had one. Mum had one, even though she'd forgotten how to use it. She rummaged through the dried-out tea bags and leftovers in the bin and tossed the cardboard and newspapers in the recycling box onto the floor smearing grey newsprint on her hands. No phone was to be found anywhere.

David Attenborough had been and gone. He loved those gibbons more than Henry loved her. She was beginning to see that now. After she had watched the local news and the horrific things going on not ten miles from her home, she was glad Henry was so wise. He was right. He was always right. London would be extremely dangerous for someone like her. He was trying to protect her. He'd told her that, time and time again.

If only they'd had a family, she thought. Henry might have been happier if she'd been able to give him a son, a boy like him, and she would have loved them both. She wouldn't have this constant, empty loneliness. She'd have been a good mother. She'd been a good administrator, too, but Henry had insisted she give up her job. Said he hadn't bought a house on the best road in Upper Swannery to watch her hightail it down the hill to St Jude's Comprehensive every day. Said the students at Rowan House were a better class: no riff-raff there with their working class, chavvy parents. She could work there if she had to have a job.

But, she wanted to say, the parents were decent if you took the time to get to know them and treated them respectfully as though they mattered. She had loved her job, had been efficient and professional. She was more than capable then. Goodness knows what had happened to her brain. What if she were going the way of her mother?

One or two colleagues had tried to keep in touch with her. They'd invited her out for drinks when there was a celebration. They'd stopped asking her in the end because she didn't answer their calls, or she let them down at the last minute. Henry would provide, he was all she needed, and he took exception to the deputy head saying he couldn't live without her.

'But he didn't mean . . . it's a turn of phrase.'

She didn't say that if Henry had paid proper attention, he would have realized she was old enough to be Marcus' mother and that Marcus was in a civil partnership with Damian, the maths teacher. She didn't go to church now, either. She'd come to understand that only impressionable, inadequate people needed to believe in a non-existent god. Time-wasting coffee mornings and gossipy knitting groups would take her away from her duties at home. That's what Henry thought. Anyway, the women there were downright bossy. They looked at him in ways he didn't like. The final nail in the coffin, he said, was when the red-haired vicar had turned up. Why wasn't she married, that's what he wanted to know. Of course, Henry was right. He always was.

The key made a quiet scraping sound. She was relieved and scared. Now she could go to bed. Henry didn't like her going up before him. She was terrified he'd notice the missing phone and think she'd hidden it deliberately. Miraculously when she returned with his coffee, it was in its cradle. She breathed a sigh of relief. Had she imagined that as well?

The next afternoon, she walked down to the bus stop, her raincoat buttoned up, and her waterproof hat pushed down over her ears – *modesty was essential in a woman her age*. Henry was taking her to an important social event. There were two hair salons in Lower Swannery but they were both managed by amateurs, Henry said. Not good enough for his wife. Not good enough for the wife of an important local dignitary. Not good enough for a professional engagement, so he had given her the bus fare to go into town. She needed to tidy herself up. Becca, her hair stylist, had been running late and had given her a coffee while she waited. That meant she had to go to the cloakroom before settling her bill. She couldn't help seeing the notice on the toilet door. It was an 0800 number and invited women-at-risk to call for a confidential chat. Was she a woman at risk? From Henry? Really? She scribbled down the number on her bus ticket just in case she should ever need it, folded it and hid it inside her powder compact, sliding it under the loose mirror.

She knew she wasn't attractive. That's why she'd been grateful when Henry had taken an interest in her. Of course, she couldn't compete with the sassy women who worked for him or the women councillors who hung on his every word (or so he said), but she could make an effort, and do her best, as Henry always said. Tonight, she was wearing her two-piece blue silk suit with sling-back shoes as instructed. He'd warned her not to say anything which might embarrass him. She knew what would happen if she did. As she fastened the jacket, she wondered if other women were scared of their husbands. All the time. Was she at risk as the notice suggested?

Henry admitted her hair was passable. He liked the scent he'd chosen for her as a birthday gift. As often happened, praise was followed swiftly by criticism. Why was she wearing a cheap, old necklace when he'd bought her a far more expensive one with diamonds and amethysts? Why did he bother to buy her tasteful things if she couldn't be bothered to wear them? And did she honestly think that much mascara was suitable for a woman her age? Heaven help her if she embarrassed him in front of his colleagues. He had a position to maintain and she'd better remember it.

She never enjoyed social events. Ever. Too many ways to fall short. She tried joining in the conversations with Henry's colleagues, but the simplest of topics left her tongue-tied and stumbling. A small wave of anger swirled around her stomach. She hadn't always been this pathetic. She knew she hadn't.

Henry paid the taxi driver and unlocked the front door. It began before she'd taken her coat off.

'What on earth did you think you were doing?' he shouted. 'Wittering on about baboons' mating habits. Don't think I didn't see you flirting with Dave Markham.'

She couldn't remember who Dave Markham was but had learned never to contradict Henry. The tiny wave of anger grew. She was aware of the thumping inside her chest. The notice on the toilet door was right. It was meant for her. She'd had enough. She would have to do something or he would control her forever. If she didn't leave him and become a person again, she would end up killing him. Or herself.

On Monday morning, Henry went to work as usual. She brushed his overcoat, polished his shoes, gave him a chaste peck on the cheek and wished him an enjoyable day. She didn't ask what she should cook for tea or say she'd see him later. After a safe interval, she picked up the phone and left a message on Heather's mobile and another on the vicar's. Then she took out her compact and dialled the 0800 number.

'My name's Audrey. I'm fifty-four years old and I'm desperate. Please, please help me.'

12. Barbara's Tuesday Evenings

As a child, I believed that people in uniform and authority were trustworthy and to be respected. Headteachers always knew best, the GP never asked our opinion and vicars were held in high esteem. We did not scrutinise professionals to see if they lived an alternative life in the shadows or had an alter ego with dodgy intentions.

Barbara dropped her keys and bag in the hallway and kicked off her flat, black pumps. She checked her watch. Half an hour before she was on call. Time for a quick shower, a change of clothes and a glass of chilled white. Twenty-five minutes later, she was sprawling on the sofa, impeccable, glossy red lipstick (*Cherry Delight*) and silver eye shadow (*Night Time Surprise*) in place, mobile fully charged. She pulled her flimsy negligee around her and hugged the bottle of Chardonnay (*Rustenberg* tonight. *Peach Garden* when she was feeling flush.) It was easier to think yourself into the part if you had the right clothes on and a glass in your hand.

The phone rang, right on cue. She left it to ring four times. Make them wait a bit.

'Well, hello there, big boy. And what can Dulcie do for you this dark, winter's evening?'

She listened to the reply. It was the same every Tuesday evening. She giggled artificially, adding appreciative and seductive murmurs. She knew she sounded like a character from a soap opera: over-acting and far from subtle. It was hard to believe that grown men like Marty (and Darryl, Owen, Archie and Guy – all booked in for Tuesday evenings) were so easily taken in by her and her insincere attention. Or perhaps they weren't taken in at all but preferred to deceive themselves that they were special rather than risking the intimacy of a relationship with a living, breathing person who might make demands on them and answer back. She was no threat to their jobs or homes, and she would keep on cashing in on their stupidity for as long as it lasted.

'What am I wearing under my dressing gown? Ooh, you cheeky, cheeky Archie!'

She paused. Timing was everything whatever anybody said. She produced the suggestive titters, moans and groans he had come to expect and for which he was paying. Twenty minutes later, Archie was gone. Satisfied or not, his time was up.

And, so the evening wore on. Barbara a.k.a. Dulcie, checked her notes. It was the same routine every week, but a slip of the tongue could be the end of a beautiful and lucrative, if artificial association. Guy was a single-minded boobs man, Marty talked dirty and Darryl just wanted to chat about his day as though she was his mother. She had no idea why he didn't just go to the pub and meet some mates. Owen was a man of few words who wanted her to talk and do stuff while he listened. Then he thanked her politely and said *the same time next week.*

She was very strict. Twenty minutes each and heaven help them if they were late. She would play the cross teacher, tell them off and describe the punishments she would inflict on them when they got home, sparing no blushes. She knew that Marty sometimes rang late on purpose and, on more than one occasion, he had begged her to meet him and carry out her threats for real. That was never going to happen. If she met any of them in the flesh, she would die a thousand deaths.

Finally, she sank into a hot bubble bath (*Restful Dreams*), washing away the smell and taste of her absent pseudo-lovers. If she were at a loose end, she'd do it all again on Thursday for cold callers. This Thursday was Parents' evening so no chance.

It had all started when she had become fascinated with her name.

'Why on earth did you call me Barbara,' she had asked her parents when she was old enough to read the Baby Names book they had left lying around.

'It says here it means warrior or foreign woman or patron saint of architects, geologists and stone masons. *His* name . . .' she pointed at her older brother, engrossed in his comic '. . . means God's gift. And you're calling *her* Jennifer. That means blessed, fair and holy. I want to be blessed, fair and holy. Not a warrior.'

Her Mum's response that they just liked the name did not appease her. Barbara was such an old-fashioned name, and it had been hi-jacked by that stupid Barbie doll with her false hair and implausible body. No. Barbara had no redeeming features whatsoever. She wanted something seductive and pretty. She made a shortlist. Serena, Melissa and Dulcie. With attention in short supply, she played with her three, new imaginary friends who called around for tea after school. What if she took one of their names and became a different person? She would have to be Barbara at school but at home she could be Melissa, Serena or Dulcie. It was a secret she and they would share.

'If you were having a baby,' she asked her nine-year old brother. 'Would you call it Melissa, Dulcie or Serena?' Nathanael stared at her. What a ridiculous question.

'I'm never going to have a baby,' he said. 'Babies are disgusting. But if I did it would be a boy called William. Or maybe Jack.'

'What if it was a girl. You can't choose.'

He gazed into the middle distance for a few seconds. 'Well, it wouldn't be Dulcie,' he said. Before he could add that it wouldn't be Melissa or Serena either, she had made her choice. She would be Dulcie. Sweet, gentle Dulcie. And nobody would know who she was even when they thought they did.

Parents' Evening was grinding on. Such a waste of time. It was a month into the school year and she, new to the school herself, was meant to have formed an opinion on the potential of twenty-four budding physicists. She could hardly remember their names, let alone predict their GCSE grades. Five minutes was more than enough to convey all that she knew about the Karens and Gareths in her class but rarely long enough to persuade pushy or anxious parents that their particular Gareth or Karen was neither doomed to certain failure nor likely to be the next Einstein.

Finally, the last appointment. She took an instant dislike to Mr Henderson who was over-assertive and felt contempt for Mrs Henderson who was an insignificant-looking woman. Bet she's called Faye or Celeste or something spineless, she thought. Barbara recognised their son, David, because of his carefully groomed, casual image, the result of hours of meticulous planning.

'Well done for coming to the after-school catch-up session,' she said, trying to get him a few Brownie points. 'He doesn't have to do that,' she added, glancing at his father.

'Yeah – well. I enjoy it, Miss,' and then, without a moment of hesitancy, a smile lurking at the corner of his lips 'Same time next week?'

Barbara's heart pounded, her palms were sweating and her vocal cords tied themselves in a knot. There was something familiar about that voice. She shuffled the papers on the desk, pretending to consult them for illuminating details. The name on the file jumped out at her, dancing around the page, gloating and haunting in equal measure: David Owen Henderson.

Owen? He was her 7:20? The one who said nothing much but was polite and listened and thanked her at the end? David Owen Henderson, her year eleven, under-age, below average GSCE student?

Barbara called in sick on Friday and laid low for the weekend. What had originally been a harmless outlet for her *alter ego*, a cheap thrill for frustrated adults and a source of pin money had become an X-rated nightmare leading, possibly to disciplinary proceedings and public humiliation. Of course, she wouldn't have signed him up if he'd told her he was a minor. Especially not a boy from her physics class. What if the others were children too?

She replayed the conversations in her head. Marty was most definitely an adult. No doubt about that; but Darryl, and Archie and Guy? What should she do? She couldn't share this, even with her best friends. She was on her own. Should she talk to Owen, ignore him, deny everything?

She could throw away the pay-as-you-go phone and delete every trace of Dulcie, or she could hold her nerve and carry on. Just be more careful. Block Owen's calls.

On Monday, she put on her best face (*Rose Blush*) and a subtle lipstick (*Pure Coral*), and walked into the physics lab as though she owned it. David aka Owen was there, waiting for her. He was acting older, almost swaggering.

'David. You're early for a Monday morning. Do you have a problem?'

'Don't know, Miss. Do you?'

She opened her laptop, wiped her hands on her trousers, turned on the screens.

'Why not tell me about it at the catch-up class tonight? 4:30 sharp.'

Even as she said it, she knew she was digging her own grave.

'Wouldn't ever be late, Miss. Know how much that upsets you.'

She walked over to the door slowly and shut it quietly and firmly

'How did you find out,' she whispered, sinking into her chair and knocking the remote control onto the floor.

'Well, Miss – or can I call you Dulcie now that we're such good friends?'

She could not control her cheeks as they turned red.

'Maybe we could discuss it on Tuesday when I call you. And maybe I'll put it on loudspeaker for all my mates to listen in.'

She raised her hands to her head. Hid her eyes.

'Wasn't sure at first. Thought I was imagining it. Everybody says boys think about sex all the time, don't they? But not during a physics lesson. Physics teachers aren't usually sexy, are they?'

How come this usually taciturn youth was suddenly so verbose and articulate?

'I couldn't say,' she began. 'I've never thought about it. I just come to school, do my job and go home again. I don't waste time wondering what year eleven boys are thinking about.'

'No? You do on a Tuesday night, Miss, don't you? It was your voice that did it. You were all excited talking about inert gases and that gave it away. And when you tore Max off a strip for being late, I knew I'd heard that tone before. Changes things a bit, don't it?'

'Yes. But not in the way you think. There won't be any more Tuesday nights. Not for you or anybody. I need you to be grown up about this and keep it between ourselves. Put it down to experience – a stupid mistake on both our parts. And in return . . .' She can't believe she is about to bribe a fifteen-year-old boy. 'Well, I'll have to think about how we get that A grade your father's so keen on. Nobody would believe an A* but we might swing an A . . .'

They both know she is talking nonsense. He snorts with contempt. 'An A grade in physics? You think I care about that? Sod my so-called father. He's not my real father and he's a controlling bastard.'

He stops abruptly when the rest of the class piles in for the first lesson. The usual banter ensues, bags are thrown on the floor, the occasional expletive is heard and lockers bang shut. Scalar and vector quantities are not the most gripping topics, especially not so this morning. The class, sensing her discomfort, takes advantage and she has never been more relieved to hear the bell at the end of the double lesson.

'Course, Dulcie,' he says when he is the only one left in the room, exaggerating the name. 'You could do something for me.'

'What's that, David,' she says as she fiddles with the computer.

'Owen. My name's Owen when I'm . . .' He kicks the table leg with his trainer. 'You're right. We should give up Tuesday nights.'

She breathes a sigh of relief. There is a God, after all.

'Until January. I'll be sixteen then. We'll skip the talking for now and move straight on, you know, to the real thing. Except I won't be paying, and it'll take more than twenty minutes. And there's one more thing you should know. My stepdad's name's Martin. How d'you think I found your number?'

13. Keith's Story

I can't tell you what a relief it was when the message came. I'd been shitting bricks for weeks, and pussyfooting around Gillian was getting beyond tedious. I'd kept her out of my bed by telling her I was the old-fashioned sort who wanted to wait until we were married. Nobody but God-botherers would say that nowadays but she settled for a few steamy kisses and a bit of a grope. I wondered if she'd changed her mind, whether being kissed wasn't all she was expecting it to be.

Her clingy, decrepit old folks were doing my head in, too, but I couldn't risk putting a foot wrong with the case hanging over me. I'd persuaded her to let them visit. It was important to pretend to be an acceptable, potential son-in-law. They'll grow to love me in time I told her.

Back to the call. The Crown Prosecution Service, said the officer grudgingly, disappointment oozing out of every word, will not be taking the matter further. He sounded like he was being forced at gunpoint to let me off even though he was sure I'd done it. The evidence is not conclusive enough to ensure a conviction. Insufficient doubt about my culpability when weighed against Ma's forgetfulness and confusion. They're not saying she might have taken the drugs herself but a jury could be persuaded.

Well! I want to shout. I'm not bloody stupid, am I? I wouldn't have bludgeoned her to death and left my prints all over the hammer. I wouldn't have smothered her with a pillow and pretended she'd had a heart attack. I wouldn't have been joining the bereavement group or eating flapjacks at the frigging book club for fun. Would I! And if you think I was a tiny smidge interested in frumpy Gillian Small, you're in the wrong job.

I don't say any of that. Of course, I don't. Instead, I do my best impression of a vulnerable, greatly relieved, grieving son. I am polite and appreciative.

'Thank you for telling me personally,' I croon. 'I am so grateful to you and your colleagues. You couldn't have been kinder.'

Then I press the red button and put the phone in my pocket. I can see Gillian in the garden through the kitchen window. She is planting bulbs It's a far cry from the crazy life she craved but she's out there every day, fully engrossed. She scours catalogues for unusual plants, checks out the habitat they need and scribbles away in her notebook, plotting where she will place everything for maximum yield. It has to look good all year round, she says. Not just in the height of summer. We want interesting, exotic plants and flowers, she says. Not borders full of boring daffs and petunias. I don't interfere. If nothing else, she's adding to the value of the property until I get rid of her, and it keeps her out of my hair now she's given up the library. She still goes back now and again to read and research and to stock up on those cheap crime stories she likes. She ought to write one, I tell her since she knows all the tricks.

She'll go all romantic when I tell her about the phone call. She'll talk about weddings and how neither of us is getting any younger and all she's wanted is a happy home and a loving husband. Well, she can have the first, temporarily. We'll see about the second. I'll wait a bit before I tell her the latest news. Let her finish the garden.

Keith never finished his story. Gillian was hysterical when the paramedics arrived and was given a sedative. Her parents were summoned and spent the night in the living room, drinking cocoa. The coroner is still considering why Keith collapsed and died suddenly and in such pain.

14. Planning Tom's Funeral

The death of a classmate has a massive effect on the peer group. They have deep feelings they can't always articulate. They want to be involved but aren't sure how, they worry it will happen to them and they are filled with guilt. Listening to them and how they choose to say goodbye to a friend is crucial if they are to cope with the loss.

They sat in the snug at *The Dog and Duck*. Marcus and Damian, Bethan and Tom's gang: Cathy, Dinesh, Dan, Becca and Paddy. It wasn't the place Bethan usually chose to discuss funerals but this was out of the ordinary. Glasses of Coke and half-eaten packets of crisps were scattered about the table. No alcohol even though one or two of them were over eighteen. Tom had left a few instructions, and Paul, Louise and the girls had shared their ideas, but they'd agreed that his friends shouldn't be left out.

'You've all been amazing,' said Bethan. 'You're not children but it's a tough call – visiting your friend's parents and cheering them up when you're in pain yourself. Not many adults can do that.'

They exchanged glances with one another, shuffled along the bench, fiddled with the crisps. They were searching for the words to respond but none came.

'I'd echo that,' said Damian. 'I don't know how you managed to sit with Tom and lark around like you did. I saw how he smiled at you all, even towards the end.'

'Yeah, well, thanks,' said Paddy. 'Doesn't bring him back though, does it?'

'Or explain why it happened in the first place,' said Dinesh. 'No offence, Rev Bethan, but your God's not so powerful now, is he?'

Cathy started crying and put her head on Dinesh's shoulder.

'I can't get away from thinking . . .' she mumbled through her tears '. . . that me and Dinesh made it worse. If we hadn't got together. I liked going out with Tom but we were seventeen. I never promised . . .'

'Most people experience guilt after a death, Cathy,' said Bethan. 'Whatever the circumstances. They tie themselves in knots wondering *what if* and *if only,* blaming themselves for all kinds of things. Nobody could have stopped this intruder in its tracks. Heaven knows the medics tried every trick in the book.'

Cathy was not convinced.

'You probably know Tom and I had conversations about how this service would go. He chose music and pictures and gave me ideas. But tell me what was special about Tom. What he liked, what he did, why you used to hang out with him.'

Nobody wanted to speak first and, in the end, they all spoke at once, laughing and crying together as they shared memories.

'D'you remember that ridiculous canal boat lift he made in year eleven? We spent hours in his bathroom trying to get it to work. Bits kept falling off but he'd just glue them back on and start again. Didn't even wait for the glue to dry before he dropped it in the water.'

'Then there was the school trip to France. He got up at night for a slash and ended up in the girls' tent . . .'

'By mistake.'

'Or so he said.'

'And how about when he dyed his hair yellow and had his ears pierced.'

'Neither of those lasted long, did they? He looked such a prat.'

'He loved his guitar. More than me, I used to think. And Rod Stewart of all people. Nobody his age should like Rod Stewart.'

'He always had a load of sweets in his rucksack. We'd eat them during boring lessons when nobody was watching.'

'Especially when we had that weird physics teacher for a bit.'

'But never during Maths, I hope,' said Damian.

'We're naming a star after him,' said Dan. 'They're sending a certificate. In time for the funeral.'

'And we've sorted all his favourite music to stream on the day. His mum said we could play it at the end while everybody's leaving.'

'Then we're having a lock-in here after the funeral. All night probably. Jo and Kate are coming.'

'We'll go out and find his star and eat sweets.'

Damian and Bethan left the group to their own devices and walked back down the road. There was nothing to say but they both valued the presence of another human being. Bethan guessed it was the first time Damian had lost a student and wondered whether his degree in education had covered bereavement. Right now, she couldn't cope with his needs. He'd have to wait his turn.

'It's not the right time for a detailed discussion,' he said as they reached the Vicarage drive. 'But when this is over, when the funeral's over, Marcus and I would appreciate a conversation with you. We're in a Civil Partnership but we'd like to get married. Tom's death has made us appreciate how unpredictable life is.'

Bethan caught her breath, frowned, sighed. She hated disappointing people.

'Always happy to chat,' she said as she smiled at him. 'No strings either way. Send me a text and we'll fix a time.'

She hated herself for giving him the slightest hope that she could marry them. Or was this the time to make a stand, push the boundaries of legality and fight their corner? After the funeral, she thought. One death was enough for now.

15. Dear Michael,

I bet you're thinking I've made up all these stories. Or that I have a vivid imagination, despite what Mrs Gane said about me in Reception class. I wouldn't blame you, and a few years ago, I'd have said the same. Until all the awful things you read about on the internet seem to be happening in your street. Well, let's not exaggerate. We haven't had bombs dropping on our foodbank queues, and no tanks have rolled across the border; but everything else has happened, more or less as I've written it, with a few embellishments. Who'd have thought a strange old woman ending her days at Bishop's Place was once a physics teacher with a risqué hobby? And that a middle-aged *librarian* should be suspected of murder.

Anyway, how are you doing? I'm glad you made it to Stratford to see your daughter. And that she booked tickets for you to see *As You Like It*. The plot is as complex as life in Swannery, and the relationships are as confusing. I hope you're following my storyline and working out who's related to whom and why. Do you remember Marcus and Damien, two teachers at the Comp? Henry, Audrey's bullying husband, used them as another excuse to goad her. Marcus was gay so unlikely to be making eyes at a woman at all, let alone one like Audrey. They were in a Civil Partnership. I got to know them better when one of the sixth-formers had a brain tumour. They were great with him.

This *is* all leading somewhere! You've been very restrained, not pestering me about why the bishop was so upset with me. I wrote a letter to *The County Herald*. You've probably googled it by now. It was around the time when the Church was discussing, again, the terrible problem of gay people and whether they could be married in church. Perish the thought! Thunderbolts might fall out of the sky if that happened. The bishops were pussy-footing around, arguing amongst themselves, threatening schism and mayhem – as they did over the debates about women bishops.

Marcus and Damian chose the wrong moment to ask me if I would marry them. They had no idea it was still impossible. To say they were stunned would be an understatement. I told them I could say some set prayers with them in church and bless them as individuals but that was the best I could offer. Even as I explained it to them, I was seething and my stomach was churning. The Church had no right to judge them and their commitment to one another. They said they'd pass, thanks. No hard feelings. So, I put my feelings into a letter to the press and I didn't mince words. The bishop's chaplain sent a Queen Victoria email. He was not amused.

Anyway, I've saved the best news until last. I've won second prize in a competition! Only a small one but still . . . and when we meet, we'll spend my winnings. £50! It won't change my life but it might stretch to two courses if you're lucky!

With love, Bethan.

PS Glad you are still using Mum's pen.

16. The Meerkat and the Warthog

Greg was Eliza Sillence's son. He was unaware that he had a half-sister buried in the churchyard, a place he had walked through on countless occasions. Little did he know that he would become a relative of baby Sara's father. His daughter's study of DNA uncovered a long-held but harmless secret, showing again the complexity of family relationships.

'Wotcher got, Sis?' mumbled Dan, shovelling cereal into his mouth and spraying milk everywhere. How old did boys have to be, thought Lizzie, before they learned to eat breakfast without sharing it with the whole family? How often would her dad have to ask somebody to put the lid back on the marmalade? Surely, by now, her teenage brother should have mastered those simple skills.

'What have I got, Dan?' said Lizzie. 'The answer to the story of our lives. This test will tell us how closely we are related to William the Conqueror, and whether our ancestors came from Iceland or Islington.'

'Hah! I can tell you where you came from for free,' scoffed Dan. 'You collected her from London Zoo, didn't you, Mum? Quarter warthog, quarter meerkat, half human. Dad wanted to send you back when he saw you.'

'Not as often as I wanted to send you back, Dan,' laughed Greg. 'And why exactly do you have a DNA kit, Lizzie? You haven't been taken in by clever marketing, have you?'

He sighed. 'You won't find any skeletons in our family closet but sometimes people have discovered things about their ancestors which might have been better left unknown.' He turned to the figures in front of him and continued jotting down numbers.

'It adds up. Mum can easily afford it. I knew she could. She's quite keen on the idea now but I'm relying on you three to support me. Say what a lovely home Bishop's Place is and how much safer she would be.'

Dan grunted. Caitlin cleared the table. Lizzie put the lid back on the marmalade.

'Come on, then, Lizzie,' said Dan, the next evening, as he mopped up the swirls of balsamic vinegar in the salad bowl, knocking petals off the flowers which drooped over the edge of the blue and white vase.

'Tell us about this DNA kit. Have you sent it back? What if you *do* discover you're descended from a meerkat and Dad has seventeen other children scattered across the country?'

'You really want to know, Danny? You think you'll be able to understand anything at all?'

''Course. I don't spend all my time playing computer games.'

'Do you have any idea what social anthropology means?'

'Try me, birdbrain.'

She grimaced. 'It'll be like explaining trigonometry to a three-year-old. Except worse.' She took the last piece of garlic bread and wiped up the remaining Bolognese sauce.

'I'm doing an optional module on population movement and ethnic diversity to help me decide if I want to pursue it for my third-year project. It's all about comparing different groups and individuals, searching for shared SNPs.'

'And the Scottish National Party is relevant because. . .?' asked Dan.

'Single nucleotide polymorphisms,' said Greg, looking up from the sports pages and pushing his plate away.

'Hey, Dad. When did you learn that?' said Lizzie.

Greg smiled. 'I have a scientific background, remember. My brain does still function, now and again.'

'Anyway, I'm starting with my roots. Then I'll sound intelligent when I sell it to my tutor. I'm going for the autosomal approach, mapping the whole genome at over 700,000 locations.'

'Whoa there. You lost me already, Sis, with your grown-up university-speak. Any idea what she's on about, Mum?'

'No, but I'm sure it will be fascinating. Maybe we should all do it. Then you'd have more to go on.'

'Good idea,' said Lizzie. 'This kind of research has huge implications for the human race. There's a database to help people find out who their biological parents are, or who the sperm donor might have been.'

'Blah! Blah! Blah!' said Dan. 'Sounds a bit dodgy to me, Sis.'

'Well *of course* I know about the issues but this is the first stage. Nothing can go wrong if it's only about me.'

'And you're not adopted, nor a criminal, you're not an unidentified body, and the single sperm donor involved was your dad,' said Caitlin.

'But she *is* still quarter meerkat and quarter warthog isn't she, Mum? Whatever anybody says.'

Three weeks later. Lizzie was sitting on the sofa, her legs curled under her, arms folded. A sheaf of papers was scattered untidily on the floor beside her.

'What's eating you, Lizzie?' yelled Dan, as he sprawled beside her. 'Even Gran's been asking me what's wrong with you.'

Lizzie squirmed, hugged a cushion to her chest.

'Sorry, Dan.'

Dan jumped. 'Now I am *really* worried. My sister is *apologising*. Oh no, the test results are out. Tell me you haven't discovered you're going to get early-onset Alzheimer's. Or you aren't my sister after all. Was I right? You're quarter meerkat, quarter warthog.'

And, after an uncomfortable silence when she failed to respond. 'You're not *pregnant*, are you? Because if you are, well, you've got options. Mum and Dad need never know.'

'No, I'm not pregnant. I'm not stupid.'

'Well, what then?'

'It's the DNA results. I've found out something awful if I'm reading it right.'

'Well, Dad knows surprising stuff. Why not ask him?'

Lizzie's face crumpled. 'No, I couldn't.'

'Why not?'

'It's about Mum. And a woman on the database.'

'What woman?' said Dan, raising his eyebrows, staring at his sister.

'Tamara Walker. She shares a range of markers with Mum.'

'You mean. . .Mum could have had a sister she didn't know about?'

'Or *we* have a sister and she didn't tell us' said Lizzie, so quietly he could hardly hear. 'This Tamara is thirty-one. Mum would have been fifteen when she had her.'

'A girl in my class had a baby when I was in year ten. Missed a whole term. Loads of teenagers get pregnant.'

'Yes, but *Mum*?'

'Slow down a bit, Sis. There could be a dozen reasons why you're wrong. I told you this stuff was dangerous.'

'Let's talk to Dad,'

'Or Mum. Or both of them.'

'When the time's right.'

The whole family was gathered for breakfast around the table their mum had rescued from the recycling centre. Caitlin was buttering toast, Dan sloshed milk onto more cereal and Greg was re-reading the Bishop's Place publicity brochure and circling key sentences. Early roses had replaced the wilting daffodils and tulips, and the marmalade jar was open. Lizzie shuffled her papers, dropping them, mixing them up.

'Dad. Mum. I need to talk about the DNA test. The results are odd.'

Greg didn't move an inch. 'Yeah, sure. Maybe later.'

'Not sure I'll be any help, but ready to listen,' said Caitlin.

'No. Now. It's important.'

The tremor in her voice made them both take notice.

'Oh, get on with it, Sis. Lizzie found a woman on the database who could be our half-sister and we're freaking out. We don't know what to do but we need the truth.'

Caitlin turned white. She put down her toast. 'And you think. . .are you suggesting Dad or I. . .have another child we haven't told you about?'

'Well, yes. No. Don't know.' Lizzie realized how unbelievable it sounded.

'Well, count me out,' said Greg. 'Unless playing with Louise Cooper in the sandpit counts as infidelity, afraid I'm boringly innocent; although there was one occasion when I held her hand as we threw bread to the ducks on the village pond.'

Lizzie and Dan looked toward their mother, not knowing who was more embarrassed.

'But hold on a minute,' whispered Greg. 'This woman; she isn't called Tamara, is she?'

'Yes. How on earth. . .'

Greg smiled at Caitlin. She brushed one hand through her hair and covered her face with the other one.

'You thought,' said Greg, half questioning, half confirming 'that Tamara was a secret love child, and Mum ... goodness me, she'd have been a child herself.'

'Fifteen', said Lizzie. 'She would have been fifteen. Can you imagine how gross it would be to think Mum had a baby and you didn't tell us?'

'More worrying that I didn't know either,' said Greg, stifling a laugh.

'It is possible to get pregnant at fifteen,' said Dan.

'Silly girl,' said Greg. 'Not you, Lizzie. Tamara. She should have known she couldn't take a DNA test and get reliable results. She didn't read the instructions properly.'

'Dad, for God's sake. Who is Tamara? Mum?'

Greg closed his eyes, moved to sit next to Caitlin, and put his arm around her.

'You know what Mum's like – always the philanthropist, rescuing old crockery from charity shops, adopting ill-treated donkeys and battery chickens. She joined the register for bone marrow donors when we were at college. I was desperate to impress her and signed up, too. And then we forgot about it.'

'But then, one day,' said Caitlin 'out of the blue, I received a letter and a test tube saying I could be a match for somebody and would I send a blood sample. We weren't expecting it to come to anything.'

'On the day we got engaged, we were told the treatment was working.'

'Isn't it all meant to be super confidential?' said Dan.

'Yes. It is. We weren't told her name for a couple more years, and only then because her parents were determined to meet the person who'd saved their daughter's life.'

'We decided not to keep in touch. It was all too emotional. I didn't want to be an angelic auntie and Tamara needed to get on with her life without a saviour in the background. Anyway, they lived miles away.'

'Mum saved a child's life, and you didn't think to tell us?' said Lizzie.

'Suppose we should have done,' said Caitlin. 'It happened long before you came along. We told Gran and Grandad, but nobody else.'

'But I still don't get how you worked it out, Dad,' said Dan.

'It's obvious, cretin,' said Lizzie, back to her old self. 'Getting foreign bone marrow affects your genetic map.

You inherit the donor's DNA. It's all on the website, but Tamara missed it. Right, Dad?'

'Something like that, Lizzie. And in case you have any doubts. . .Mum and I have been together for more than twenty-five years and there are no long-lost half-siblings anywhere. And, please, please, will somebody put the lid back on the marmalade.'

17. Eliza's Story

Eliza has never forgotten her secret love child, nor the child's
father who was unaware of her existence. The memory lived
like a seed deep within her heart and mind.

Greg said she had a fetish, that she was weird and it was
unnatural to spend hours close to the bones and ashes of
the dead, making up stories about the poor devils whose
remains were buried under the buttercups and dandelions.

'They're laid to *rest*,' he said. 'They don't want to be
disturbed, especially not by a stranger.'

'No, you're wrong. Nobody wants to be forgotten.
Anyway, I'm not a stranger. I come to speak to Dad.'

'Dad's dead, Mum. He can't hear you. It's been ten
years.'

Eliza loved the afternoons she spent in St. Jude's Garden
of Remembrance. Tucked away off the busy path leading
from the shops to the library, it was a sanctuary, a place
to think. It was her secret garden. Greg said that was
ridiculous because she was always saying how many
people she saw there but that wasn't the kind of secret she
meant. Every season had a distinctive flavour. Elderflower,
cherry blossom, winter jasmine, the first cut of the grass in
the spring and the aftertaste of autumn rain.

There were two conveniently placed wooden benches,
perfect for getting your breath back and resting your legs.
Engraved brass plates revealed they had been given in
memory of *"Louis, our brave hero"* and *"Prudence Wainwright,*

the best wife and cook ever." Every Tuesday and Thursday afternoon, summer or winter, after she'd listened to the Archers, she would tuck her wispy, grey hair under her creased, felt hat, put on her cardigan or raincoat, and walk to the church, stopping to rest on her walking frame every few minutes. The strap of her canvas handbag went right over her head and across her body, safe and secure like the community police officer had told them when she'd come to the Knit and Natter meeting. You never knew who might be waiting for an unsuspecting, elderly woman to come along with a bag carelessly dangling from one shoulder. Eliza had never seen anybody who resembled a potential assailant, but it was sensible to take proper care.

She would choose a bench, either Louis' or Pru's, depending on the sun and the direction of the wind. From Louis' bench, she could see Joe's memorial stone which reminded her, as if she could forget, that he had *Died 17th May 2010* and was *Beloved husband to Eliza and loving father to Gregory.* She would pull off any stray leaves, brush away the spiders' webs and trace the letters with her finger before chatting to him about her day.

If she sat on the best cook's bench, she could enjoy the changing colours of the huge oak tree in the vicarage garden and see everybody rushing down the path: pushchairs and bicycles, children on scooters, pensioners arm-in-arm, gardeners with watering cans, women with library book bags. The whole world came out after lunch, but few had time to sit and rest and enjoy the smells and sounds. From there, she could talk to *Sara Eliza. Born 5th June 1956. Died 6th June 1956.* Several decades had passed but she still had to wipe away a tear and blow her nose as she whispered 'Hallo, precious one.' Funny to think of Joe and Sara lying beside each other but never meeting. Not in this life, anyway.

She breathed deeply, content because she was close to the two people she had loved and lost. She had loved Sara's father for a while but that was different. Of course, she loved Greg, too. Of course, she did but he was still very much alive. She could see him any day she chose.

She knew Greg wanted to put her in a home. He kept bringing it up in conversation, talking about his friend's parents and how settled they were in Bishop's Place with their own front door and microwave. He left brochures lying around and told her money was no object, he'd done the maths. House prices were booming. If she sold the bungalow, she could live comfortably for the next twenty years. He didn't say it would be a miracle if she lived anything like that long. It would be better for her, he said, and it wasn't right she had to manage on her own.

Eliza wasn't worried about moving into a home if she had her privacy and could take all her treasures with her as long as she wasn't forced to play bingo or make flowers out of tissue paper or pretend to like people when they had nothing in common. She knew it made sense. She could imagine living in a roomy bedsit at Bishop's Place. The bungalow had been ideal when Joe was alive because he could turn his hand to anything, but it was in serious need of attention now. She was tired of cleaning and polishing when there was nobody to notice. She couldn't reach to change the light bulbs, and though she had money in the bank, you couldn't get a man in for every little chore.

But Bishop's Place was on the edge of town, too far to walk. She couldn't leave the garden of remembrance and couldn't tell Greg why. It had been hard enough telling Joe, way back when. Had taken all the courage she had but she knew she mustn't walk down the aisle harbouring a secret.

It wasn't as though she'd been disloyal to him. They hadn't met until her twenty-first birthday, five long years after she'd borne and buried her baby, but she'd been worried he'd be horrified and leave her.

She had taken his arm and walked him down the path into the memorial garden. There were no benches then, but she'd guided him to the stone, still clean and fresh. He'd been delighted to stop for a quick kiss, but she held him at arm's length and said 'This is Sara Eliza. My daughter. If you want your ring back, I'll understand.'

He didn't raise his voice or push her away. Barely flinched, though she could see the tiny muscles in his jaws working away. She could hear his breathing, in, out, in, out, as though he were playing for time.

'Tell me about her,' he said and she had known it would all be all right.

'Billy was the youngest Belvoir boy.'

Joe had shifted from foot to foot, put his hands in his pockets, took them out again.

'We bumped into each other, literally, one bonfire night. I'd gone with my friends and he'd come with his brothers. He'd stayed in the army when the war ended and was home on leave.'

'And he forced himself on you,' said Joe, gripping her hand. 'Typical posh boy.'

'No. It wasn't like that. I was sixteen and I was flattered. He was much older than me. He was so, so *confident*. I knew we had no future but it didn't matter. *You never know where I'll be posted next*, he'd said. *Just because the war's over. I'm still in the army* and we, we, you know.'

Joe did know. All too well.

'He used to buy me sweets, sherbet lemons. He said the fizz reminded him of me, bubbly and alive. It was all over in a fortnight. Billy went back to his base and that was that.'

'What I'd do to him if I had the chance,' snarled Joe, pulling her close towards him. He smoothed her hair with his broad, carpenter's hands. 'And what about your mum and dad? What did they have to say about it?'

'I kept it hidden for as long as I could. I didn't want anybody to make me get rid of her. It would have to be adopted, Dad said.' She shivered, remembering the grief she had carried along with the baby.

'They sent me to stay with my auntie. When the baby started coming, too early, I thought I was going to die. She was tiny and blue, and she sounded like a kitten. I spent all night trying to feed her but she was dead by morning. I called her Sara. My little princess.' Joe gave her his handkerchief and wiped his own eyes on his sleeve.

They were married in St. Jude's in October 1961. They had eight black and white photographs in an album with silver writing on the front, and one picture was of Eliza standing beside the memorial stone with the oak tree in the background. Their secret.

And now she had to work out what to tell Greg. She wanted to chat to Joe about it, but as she approached the garden, she saw both benches were in use. Clusters of children with clipboards and pencils were gathered around one, their brows furrowed in concentration. Seemed like only yesterday Greg was that size, pulling up his grey socks, his thin legs dangling out of his shorts like drainpipes, his stripy tie halfway down his shirt.

A woman wearing a trench coat and a red beret was sitting on Louis' bench. Eliza stopped in her tracks, unused to company, and played with her buttons while she thought about what to do. She couldn't go home, not without a rest. When Father Dominic was vicar, she used to sit in the church porch. You could have sat there for a week and not seen a soul. Now there was a woman vicar with ginger hair. Friendly enough but far too energetic. There were all kinds of goings on. Alpha courses, Messy Church, missional lunches, whatever they were. Rivers of poppies. And always a stream of individuals fiddling with the noticeboards, rearranging furniture or huddling in groups, heads down and voices hushed. There was a huge TV screen inside the new glass door with announcements and photos on an endless loop. It made her head ache.

She would have to be brave and join Red Beret. There was enough room, after all. The woman sensed her hovering and moved along to one end of the bench. They exchanged shy, embarrassed glances.

'Sorry,' said Eliza. 'I had to sit down. And the children are busy on the other bench.'

'Don't apologise,' said Red Beret. 'I'm glad of the company. I'm Faye.'

'Mrs Sillence. Eliza. You are vaguely familiar, but I don't remember seeing you here before.'

'I drop in occasionally at weekends. When I get time. You'll think I'm silly but I like to talk to Mum.' She nodded towards the edge of the memorial garden and a polished stone. It was too far away for Eliza to read the words.

'Mum died in London, but her ashes are buried here. Dad always planned to move back and eventually, he did. He was useless without her. And now he's not very well, but we've finally persuaded him to move into the retirement home where I work. Bishop's Place. Do you know it?'

Eliza nodded. 'My friend Isobel's there now. It's so sad. She forgets what day of the week it is; can't remember her name most days.'

'Dad was adamant he wouldn't move unless we promised to bring him here once a month on a Sunday afternoon. Then he can be close to Mum again. There's space for him next to her when the time comes.'

Eliza nodded. 'My Joe's over there. I talk to him, too.'

'I think about the lives of the people on the gravestones,' said Faye. 'Make up stories about them. *Clara Maria died 1930 aged 69. Edwin died 1950 aged 90.* Poor Edwin. Twenty years on his own.'

'Or maybe it was lucky Edwin,' said Eliza. 'Perhaps Clara nagged him and he was glad to see the back of her; maybe he put something in her tea.'

'And what about *Ethel, 1894 – 1934 loving mother of Sissy, Fred, Jim, Bill, Ellen, Jessica, and Pete.* Seven children! No wonder she was dead by the time she was forty. And this one always has me in tears. *Sara Eliza.* One day old.'

They sat, in silence. Kindred spirits. She was kind, this woman with her red beret and long brown boots. Warm and friendly.

'She's mine,' said Eliza. 'Sara Eliza is my daughter.'

Red Beret took a deep breath, gasped, and stuttered incoherently.

'It's fine,' said Eliza, surprised at how easy it was to talk. It was like she'd known this woman for years.

'I'm glad to tell you. Makes her important though she only lived for a few hours. Nobody else knows. Not now Joe's dead.'

She shuffled around on the bench, checking her bag was safe.

'My son, Greg, bless him, thinks I'm barmy coming here to talk to Joe. Can't imagine what he'd say about having a half-sister.'

'Especially since you talk to her as well!' Red Beret pulled her coat around her, crossed her legs, waited.

'He wants me to go into Bishop's Place, too. Says it's full of interesting people. Says it makes sense. He means well but he's a pharmaceutical research scientist.' She said it as though it explained everything.

'What about you? What do you want to do?'

Eliza sighed and looked down at the tiny memorial. 'I don't mind. I'm ready to move.'

'But you can't leave Joe or Sara.' It was more of a statement than a question.

Eliza nodded and blew her nose, offering her new friend a sweet from the paper bag crumpled in her pocket.

'Ooh, lemon sherbets. My Dad loves these. Eats them all the time. Says they were his childhood favourites.'

As they returned to the path, Faye paused at a memorial stone on the other side of the hedge. 'Bye for now Mum.' She blew a kiss. Eliza read the script. *Ellen Keziah Belvoir, beloved wife of William and mother to Titus and Faye.* For a moment, she lost her balance and gripped the walking frame. Faye clung to her arm.

'Steady. You look like you've seen a ghost.'

'It's such an unusual name,' she muttered, trying to make light of her shock. 'I once knew a man called Belvoir. What a coincidence. Anyway, he was called Billy.'

'Everybody used to call Dad Billy. Until he was promoted. He thought William sounded more professional.'

On the next two Sunday afternoons, Eliza struggled to her secret garden. She convinced herself she needed the exercise, and it had nothing to do with the slim chance she might bump into Faye and her father. In case it was the same Billy. She didn't care one way or the other if it was or wasn't. Theirs had been a brief relationship of the moment. Nothing more, nothing less. She had never told him about the baby.

She brushed her hair and chose a clean blouse and a scarf which Joe had told her brought out the silvery-blue of her eyes. It was busier than during the week. There were people in and out of the church and dads with children on their way to the adventure playground. She was exhausted by the time she made it back home.

On the third Sunday, she couldn't go because Greg, Caitlin and the children came with a roast dinner ready to reheat and a glossy brochure advertising the newly refurbished suites at Bishop's Place. *A real home from home* was emblazoned across pictures of smiling women with white teeth and a man wearing a cardigan and holding a garden trowel.

'Before you say anything, Greg,' she said as they stood in the kitchen balancing pots and baking trays and before she could change her mind, 'I've been thinking and you're right. It's time to sell up and move into a home. As long as you're sure to tell the King my change of address for the telegram.'

There were conditions, though. She would go when the right room became available and if she could take her treasures with her; and there were things she had to talk to him about but not today.

Greg was so shocked he nodded like a lucky Chinese cat. Caitlin said how sensible she was, and it was what Joe would have wanted, and they all had her best interests at heart. 'How about we leave the new brochure for you to browse through later?'

The next Sunday, she gave herself a talking-to as she shut the front door and adjusted her bag strap. 'You are not a teenager, Eliza Sillence. Stop behaving like one. You loved your husband and you've had a long and happy life. It may not be the same Billy. It was a long time ago. It was a mad fling. Nothing more.'

As she rounded the bend, she recognised Red Beret waving to her across the grass.

'Mrs Sillence. Eliza. Over here.'

Faye was sitting on Pru's bench. Two men were with her. One must be her husband, the one bending down with a brush. The other one was in a wheelchair, slightly built and hunched up, wrapped in a thick overcoat and knitted scarf. Eliza waved back and walked over slowly, trying to recognise the energetic man of her youthful dreams in the small, elderly figure. She spotted the military badge on his lapel.

'What a nice surprise,' said Eliza.

'Dad, this is Mrs Sillence. Eliza. We met in the garden a few weeks ago. Eliza likes talking to people, too, even if they are dead.'

Don, Faye's husband, stood up, and shook hands, brushing cobwebs from his trousers. Billy half turned his head.

''Excuse me if I don't get up. Bit unsteady nowadays.'

'Me, too, Billy,' said Eliza. 'Fancy a sherbet lemon?'

18. David's Story

The procreation of children is a complex issue. On the one hand, unwanted pregnancies may lead to heartache. Not every child is treated as a precious and special gift. On the other hand, failure to conceive is a debilitating and terrible problem for those who are desperate for a child.

David and Nicki sat holding hands. They were in the senior consultant's office on the fifth floor of the university hospital's all-singing, all-dancing private wing. Three computers with swirling, blue and green screensavers dominated the space, while charts and pictures of various parts of the human anatomy filled the notice boards. Mr Wilson was kind but matter-of-fact.

'Can you run that by me again?' asked David.

'You have a rare, genetic condition called *azoospermia*. It means you are producing no sperm.'

David sat, massaging his biceps as though he might find and wake a few sleepy swimmers there. He could feel his cheek muscles twitching. He knew Nicki would see how nervous he was.

'Can't you do anything about it?' said David.

'We could hunt for sperm and see if we can harvest a few. But we don't think that will work in your case and I don't want to give you false hopes.'

'No. Thank you. I'd rather know the truth. It's hopeless, then. This is the end of the line.'

'I can offer you other options,' said Mr Wilson. 'Let's talk them through and then I can refer you for a counselling appointment in a couple of days.'

Everybody at the clinic was at pains to say it was a *shared challenge* and allotting blame was unhelpful. David didn't need anyone to blame him. He could do that well enough himself. He'd promised Nicki everything. All she'd wanted was a family, the one thing he couldn't give her.

Swannery, he'd told her, would be the perfect place to bring up children which is why they'd moved there. They had tried every different way of having sex. Early in the morning, late at night, standing up, sitting down. In fact, he'd joked, they were more versatile than the Kama Sutra. Nothing had worked. Desperation and routine displaced pleasure and passion. Somehow, being obliged to do it, made it less like being in love and more like an exercise in mechanical engineering. A problem with his equipment was ironic, given how much time he spent honing his muscles and keeping fit, trying to look his best. He'd met Nicki as an undergrad on the banks of the Cam. She was a looker all right, but he had no time for a relationship. His energy was directed towards keeping his place in the first eight. A couple of months later he realized he was scanning the towpath for her when he should have been listening to the cox. Focus, focus! he told himself. Neither Hugo nor Will had made it into the famous blue boat. If he could achieve that, he would have one up on them. Finally. Then he would ask Nicki out.

In the end, he won his place, earned his colours and rowed in the Boat Race. Oxford beat them by a length but he'd still been proud. At the ball, Nicki had forced his hand and more or less made a pass at him. Said she was sorry they'd lost. Right now, and years later, he'd swap every cup and medal in his cabinet and the right to be called a Cambridge Blue for a few lively swimmers. But this was the one bit of his body he could do nothing about.

The next week, he visited his father unannounced, when he knew his mother was babysitting for his brother. To put it crudely, he said, he had the balls but no live ammunition. He was firing blanks and always would be. There was no explanation for why he, rather than his brothers or anybody else, had taken this particular hit, but there was no way on earth he would be making a baby. His dad listened, put his arm around his son, and said nothing.

Nicki had blurted everything out in a message to her parents so he wasn't surprised when they offered to pay for a long, exotic holiday to *help take your mind off it*. David had to take the phone from her before she shouted at them.

'It's not a passing misfortune to be made better with an indulgent treat,' she ranted.

'It's their way of helping,' David had said. 'It's all they can do. Maybe we'll enjoy it.'

They went to the Maldives. David took the consultant's report with him. He waited until Nicki was in the spa before slipping it from his suitcase. When he'd read it from cover to cover again, twice, he wandered off to the beach, untied a dinghy, and withdrew to the privacy of the sea where he rowed for all he was worth. There must be a solution. There always was. There was nothing wrong with Nicki so they could use a sperm donor, but whenever he thought about that, he felt sick in the pit of his stomach. How could he spend nine months watching Nicki carrying a stranger's child? What if the stranger tracked their child down in twenty years, or the baby was ugly, slow or unlovable? If their daughter was pregnant when she was thirteen or their son did drugs, who would they blame then? Trawling through a catalogue searching for a prime, male candidate … well, it was demeaning. It was more like hiring a stud than creating a family.

They loved the hotel and the tropical garden and marvelled at the blue skies, turquoise water, and lush palm trees. They snorkelled, sailed and did some scuba diving. They even had sex for pleasure. But the pain was still there when the holiday came to an end. They brought it back to Swannery with their souvenirs and dirty washing. David arrived home after his first day back at the office to find Nicki still in her work clothes sitting on a stool at the breakfast bar. When she raised her head, her eyes were red and puffy.

'How was your day?' He wasn't sure if he wanted to know.

'Craig's wife is expecting a boy. Another one. They're disappointed because they wanted a girl.'

David grimaced. Plonked himself down next to her. He had spent much of the day fielding Henry Bull's constant complaints. His irritating colleague fancied himself as an indispensable asset whose every word should be obeyed. In between, David had caught up with clients and avoided meaningful conversation with anybody, not even Jamie, his best mate. Now he surveyed the kitchen. Several bags and boxes were scattered around the floor and on the breakfast bar.

'I did a shop at lunchtime. Gave me an excuse not to talk to anybody. Couldn't be bothered to cook proper food. Now I can't be bothered to put it away.'

'Yeah. Easy to get used to being waited on, isn't it? And it's so bloody cold.'

He glanced at her laptop. Beautiful babies and smiling couples with perfect white teeth. It was the website of a clinic in San Francisco. A clinic specialising in male infertility. He moved the bags from the counter to the floor and pulled up the stool next to her. Avoiding his eyes, she scrolled down and let him read the blurb.

'It's desperation, Nicki. We know all this stuff. It'd be fine if there was a blockage, a weak sperm count, or an abnormality. But you heard the consultant. He can find nothing. Zilch. Not a tiny, weeny, inadequate tiddler hiding amongst the rocks. How can anybody help? Even a cutting-edge guru in the U.S. with jet black hair and immaculate teeth.'

'But we *have* always wanted to go to San Francisco, haven't we? What's to lose?'

Quite a lot, he didn't dare say: time, money, energy, dignity, hope. He shrugged, wondering how long they could go on like this. They had to face the truth. They would never produce a baby.

'Anyway, before you go spending all our Air Miles, let's think about other options.'

Nicki responded well to a business-like approach. She loved nothing more than a spreadsheet and tapped away. It would give them a semblance of control. He'd done his research. Infertility issues often led to divorce. He'd asked himself whether, if he loved Nicki, he would set her free to find a man with a half-decent sperm count. Wondered if that's what she wanted but didn't have the guts to say. He wasn't going to be the one to suggest it. He'd agree to a sperm donor before he'd agree to a split.

'Well, there's always divorce,' said Nicki, winking, half-smiling. 'Easiest option.'

'Sure. If you want. As long as I get to keep the house. And the beer fridge.'

She threw a pack of bagels at him which he caught, grateful that she was smiling.

'Using a sperm donor is complicated,' he said. 'One man can father hundreds of children. Thousands. Our baby could have half sisters and brothers all around the world. There have been some real charlatans doing all kinds of immoral and illegal things.'

'Yes, but not now,' said Nicki. 'Back in the day, maybe. Everything's regulated now. In this country anyway.'

'Maybe. How could we be sure, though? And imagine going to parents' evening and scrutinizing every kid to see if they had the same colour hair or turned up nose as ours did.'

They sat in silence, not sure where to go next. David reached across and scrolled up and down the website himself. Then he revisited the spreadsheet and gave the laptop back to her. She coloured in three columns, red, green, and yellow.

'Phone a friend?'

Over my dead body, he thought but didn't say, in case it gave her ideas. He listened while she rattled off all their male associates. Family members on Nicki's side were first to be struck off the list.

'There's a reason why it's illegal to marry your brother or first cousin,' David said. 'And don't even think about my brothers. When we had everybody over for Sunday lunch our child wouldn't know whether to call Hugo uncle or daddy.'

Every friend fell short. Wrong-shaped face, a bit selfish, not clever enough, no creativity, lifelong smoker, weird mother, too religious.

'I married *you*,' said Nicki. 'For better for worse, forsaking all others. Let's make a call to San Francisco. There's nothing to lose.'

David was thankful that nobody else had passed muster. He glanced at the screen again. The Californian superhero's smiley face kept popping up like an advert for expensive orthodontic treatment. Perhaps it was worth scanning the report and sending it. Nicki wouldn't rest until she'd exhausted every avenue. He was hoping she'd be convinced by a definitive no. He'd had enough prodding and poking to last a lifetime.

Mr White Teeth confirmed what David had known all along. The private report was comprehensive. Unless there had been a clinical error, no San Francisco superhero could make David fertile. They would be better 'exploring other avenues.'

'How about praying for a miracle?'

'Like a virgin birth, you mean. Like God's sitting there waiting for you to get in touch when there's been radio silence for the last twenty-five years; and is going to leap into action and send a tiny messenger with special powers.'

Adoption was the safest, cleanest, and least painful route. They would be equal partners, share the risks and be certain the child was theirs for all time. Thankfully, the spreadsheet agreed.

19. Baked Beans and Toothpaste

Fiona was the third member of the MAFIA. Not a name I used though she and Magda hadn't made it easy for me in the early days. Audrey had tagged along and been labelled by association and I'd known as soon as I met them that they would have interesting stories but I wasn't expecting this.

'It's so long ago,' said Fiona. She'd been changing her mind about the new vicar. Knew she should make an effort, invite Bethan to tea. They sat in the cluttered conservatory surrounded by geraniums and ferns, watching the water feature do its desultory best. Fiona described herself as a *woman with a fuller figure, protected from the winter cold by an extra layer or two of padding.* She had puffy pink cheeks and a large mole on the right side of her chin. Her old-fashioned chignon was held in place by a black ribbon and tortoiseshell comb.

'It's more than fifty years ago now. It's hard to believe, but it still makes me shiver.'

'With rage or anxiety?'

'Both! It was my first job and nobody else had noticed what was going on. They were too busy trying to impress, too old to make waves, or saw what they wanted to see. Somebody must have known what he was doing.'

'Maybe they were scared. It was different then, wasn't it?'

'Oh yes.' Fiona seemed desperate to tell her story, defend her territory, and explain the way she was. She fiddled with her bracelet, twisting it around her wrist again and again. 'You knew your place and stayed in it, especially if you were a woman until called up higher by a man in authority. Anyway, it would have been easier to challenge God than the headmaster. It would be his word against mine and you can guess who would win.'

'Not the newly qualified recruit fresh from college.'

'Exactly.'

Fiona's parents had moved out of London after the war. They brought with them an edgy attitude and were ambitious to better themselves, giving Fiona the opportunities they had missed. She fulfilled their dreams by going to college and qualifying as a teacher. Her first job was at Swan Meadows Primary School, a post-war flagship school, symbolic of hope and peace and all that was good and true. She was to teach 1A.

'That's year three now,' she explained.

The school secretary, Miss Jackson, who wore pearls and twin sets in anaemic, pastel colours, was at the centre of everything.

'She was full of herself,' said Fiona. 'She was always going on about the posh *School for Young Ladies* she attended when we all knew the girls who went there were the ones who couldn't get into the High. But she was a fount of knowledge and knowledge is power.'

'Useful but annoying,' said Bethan, thinking of Magda.

Fiona nodded, and squeezed the lemon into the Earl Grey, inhaling the fragrance of the citrus fruit.

'She ran around after Mr Goodman pandering to his every need. The sun shone from every orifice, but if I'd been older and wiser, I would have got her on my side earlier.'

Sounds familiar thought Bethan. Good plan.

'Then there was dear old Mr Thant, the caretaker. He was Burmese. Came over after the war and never left. He was always friendly, pottering about in his blue boiler suit and moccasins, a bucket and mop in his hand. Now and again, I'd catch him staring at me from a distance in a distracted way.'

'Do you think he knew?'

'Definitely. He was sizing me up. Deciding if he could trust me. Nobody was going to listen to him, were they – a cleaner and a foreigner? Except Mr Matthews Jr did. He was the chair of governors' son,' said Fiona, her cheeks reddening. 'I carried a torch for the younger Mr Matthews for ages. If I'd been braver. . .'

Fiona described Mrs Waterman, who should have gone to prison for aiding and abetting. She was old. Pushing forty. She had wispy, dyed hair and pointed features and drove a blue and white Triumph Herald. Her baby daughter, Emily, was a late surprise, a blessing or a mistake, nobody knew. She and Mr Goodman used to drive to work together with the baby sitting on her lap in the front seat. Yes, really. Long before the Clunk-Click-Every-Trip campaign.

'Everybody knew the Goodmans and the Watermans were close friends. They went out for dinner every payday. We couldn't afford to do that. People talked about them and suggested there was more to it, but nobody ever caught them at it. And what was wrong with colleagues enjoying steak and chips, and strawberry gateau.'

'What was he like, this Mr Goodman? He didn't live up to his name, by all accounts.'

'He was terrifying. Far too handy with the cane. Short and lithe and ferret-like. His wife, Sylvia, was head at another school. Glamorous and well-groomed, she was. Goodness knows what she saw in him. She wore chunky gold necklaces, bracelets and expensive dresses which didn't come from Reg's market stall.'

'Hardly a crime. What on earth happened? It must have been serious if you're still affected by it. And you're not alone. Whenever his name comes up, I get rueful looks and nervous laughter from anybody over sixty.'

'Yes, it's weird. He's been dead for years but it makes no difference. The first day I was there, I watched him scoop some coins from the school fund bag, give it to a prefect and send her across the road to the newsagents to buy him cigarettes. I was about to challenge him, but he glared at me, daring me to speak. When I asked. Mrs Jackson about it, she said he was showing trust in the top class, giving them responsibility.'

'They'll be going to senior school next year, remember,' she'd said, concentrating on her typewriter. 'I expect he put a pound note in and was taking out the change.'

'But they had to cross the main road. They should have been in class, and they were eleven years old, for God's sake.'

'Not to mention the evils of smoking and the bad example he was setting them.'

Fiona nodded, sipped her tea, and paused for breath.

'They didn't know it caused cancer then, to be fair, but that was the tip of the iceberg. A couple of weeks later, we were planning the harvest festival. He was obsessive about every detail and made a great fuss about what the children should bring. I thought he was trying to impress the governors.'

'Weren't they all well-meaning upstanding, middle-aged women in wide-brimmed hats in those days?'

'And men in tweed jackets who handed out sweets and certificates and were patronising and genial,' said Fiona. Too genial to suspect Goodman? 'Turns out they were cleverer than they looked.'

Every class would participate, and every display board be decorated. Older children would recite harvest poems, the infants would paint pictures. Fruit and veg would brighten up the stage, to be distributed later to the poor and needy by the vicar. And, in a new venture, we would collect toiletries: toothpaste, soap, shampoo, which would be taken to a men's mission for ex-servicemen for whom we should show grateful and respectful sympathy. None of us asked why we couldn't give it to the poor who lived up the road, not half a mile from the school.

'Jesus visited the sick, the hungry, and the poor,' Mr Goodman told the assembled children, many of whom came to school without breakfast, 'and it is our duty to be kind and loving and give generously.'

'But Jesus didn't hide stuff in his loft, did he,' said Fiona. 'Stuff he didn't need.'

Pulling dead leaves off the geraniums, she continued the saga. After Easter, Mr Thant came into his own, marching up and down with his special machine – touch it at your peril – painting white lines all over the field. Sports Day was coming. Eggs and spoons, sacks, hoops, and ropes were retrieved from the storage shed. Hurdles were mended, sand raked and the starter pistol oiled and tested. The top year had done their exams by now, said the head and everybody could relax.

A pile of purple-smudged newsletters for parents appeared in the staff room. Any child not competing in the races had to buy a six-penny ticket to attend, and attendance was compulsory. Parents would pay a whole shilling.

'Is that legal?' Fiona had asked the omniscient Mrs Jackson. 'More to the point, is it moral? Some families on the Lower Swannery estate have five or six kids.'

It won't do your career any good to challenge the headmaster on everything. She could still hear the self-important school secretary in full flow. *You're on probation, remember. It's all for a good cause.* And which good cause would that be, she'd wondered?

Mums were talking at the school gate, sharing a rumour that Michelle had got from Ivy who'd heard it from Pat whose brother worked at the town hall. Mr Goodman was being taken to court for stealing jewellery. When had he stolen it, and from where? Surely, he could afford to buy his wife all the jewellery she wanted and, come to think of it, she did have an awful lot.

Rather than be caught on the back foot, Mr Goodman went on the offensive in a self-deprecating way, as if he found the joke even funnier than they did. He wrote a clear statement which was read to the staff at the weekly meeting, to pupils in assembly, and then sent to parents in a special edition newsletter headed *Headmaster Goes to Court.*

He had been summoned to court, he wrote, to serve on a *jury*, not for stealing *jewellery*. Enunciating vowels was important. Mrs Jackson would never have made such a mistake. He would be away for a week and back in time for Sports Day. And how amusing it was some people had misunderstood.

'While he was away,' said Fiona, speaking more quickly as she relived the events, 'we took our chance, Mr Thant, Mr Matthews, and myself. We've five days, I told them. I can see us now walking the bounds of the playing field pretending to discuss the finer points of the relay race.'

Mr Matthews Jr said his dad had been suspicious for a while; he'd been trying to get his hands on the accounts and had an appointment with the bank that very afternoon.

'For a moment, I thought he fancied me and that he was going to make a move.' Fiona gazed out of the conservatory window at the single weeping pear tree in the middle of the garden.

'Mr Thant had a friend working at the mission, another caretaker. He got in touch and found out more. Mrs Goodman's school was collecting for the same cause. For the price of a box of Good News chocolates, Mr Matthews Snr acquired all the accounts books for the last six months from Mrs Jackson. It was her memory, her detailed knowledge of the workings of the school which proved to be most helpful. She wouldn't lie to the police, even for Mr Goodman. They came in, charmed and scared her in equal measure while Mr Goodman and his fellow jurors were busy weighing up innocence and guilt on the scales of justice.'

'It's almost unbelievable.'

'Most normal people would think so, but a few nail-biting weeks later, Mr Goodman was arrested in the school playground and his wife in her school car park as she was loading her boot with baked beans and toothpaste.'

'It's still unbelievable!'

'It was rumoured their lawyers told them to plead insanity,' said Fiona. 'I think they were joking, but it might have served them better. The arguments for the defence were non-existent. There were piles of stuff in their garage and loft. They'd stolen it all from the families of children they were meant to be educating. They couldn't have used it all if they'd lived to be a hundred. And they couldn't plead poverty. That's what hurt most. Many families were living on the breadline.'

'In one way nothing changes,' said Bethan. 'We still have queues for the foodbank every Tuesday morning. It wasn't the thieving that was the worst thing, was it? It was who they'd stolen from.'

'And that they were in authority, people to be trusted, role models for young minds.' She took an embroidered handkerchief from her cardigan pocket. 'Like Father Dominic.'

They sat in silence, a new level of understanding between them.

'I was treated like a pariah for a bit,' said Fiona. 'I knew we'd done the right thing but it took six months to get the case to trial and I had to stand in the witness box and answer endless questions. I was terrified. Even more terrified he'd get away with it. My career would have been over.'

'I can imagine. I went through the same when the *County Herald* published my article on the state of the Church of England. I wrote it and I sent it in. I can't blame anybody but myself. Loads of people agreed with me but didn't have the guts to say it out loud or write it in black and white. I'm afraid my bishop took it rather badly, though it wasn't addressed to him personally.'

'Exactly, Bethan. I'd be called a whistleblower now. And I was proved right. When they were sent down for five years, I was ecstatic but then as soon as the adrenalin stopped pumping, the stress and strain became overwhelming. Believe it or not, some people still blamed me for speaking out, even after seeing the photos of his loft and all the boxes and tins. Even after he'd been convicted. I finished the year and took some time out, but, in the end, I had to leave. Moved into secondary and taught domestic science. I don't think I was popular there either. There was a physics teacher called Barbara. Gave me the creeps. Something disturbing about the way she talked to the children. Especially the boys.'

'You're a right Miss Marple, aren't you?' said Bethan.

Fiona smiled. Smoothed the creases in her skirt. She didn't like compliments, if such it was.

'I'd learned my lesson. Kept my mouth shut. I couldn't risk another disaster.

'And Mr Matthews Jr? What happened to him?'

'He married Miss Jackson. Apparently, he preferred old-fashioned women. I never met anybody else. At least, no one I could trust. It made me think twice about men. Particularly, the ones in authority. And d'you know what? Nobody ever found out what happened to all the baked beans.'

20. Amelia's Flowers

Even the most professional people can have blind spots and make bad judgements. Harriet was dissatisfied with the way the justice system was working and lost all sense of reason as she tried to take over the case from the sidelines.

'Damn, damn and damn, again.' Harriet dropped her briefcase on the floor and ran her fingers through her unruly crop. She slammed the fridge door shut, rattling the ice dispenser. Then she poured herself a generous gin and tonic and tossed the newspaper across to Roger.

'I don't know what's got into Godfrey. Anybody can see Stephen Bailey is an abusive, manipulative, and dangerous bastard. A typical repeat offender.'

'Don't hold back,' said her husband, adding a lemon slice to her glass. 'Say what you're really thinking.'

Harriet knew Roger would forgive the outburst. It was her passion that had attracted him to her in the first place.

'Sometimes, you just have to accept the law is an ass,' he said.

'But the judge doesn't have to be, for God's sake. Any half-wit can see what's happened. Bailey's solicitor has persuaded a wet behind-the-ears social worker to dig up dodgy stats from the States showing there's a 1% chance of that poor baby *not* having been shaken to death and they've convinced everybody it was *an unfortunate and unexplained tragedy*. What bollocks.'

'Didn't you say Bailey's prison report was exemplary, and there was medical evidence backed up by new research? And why exactly are you getting involved?'

Harriet ignored the questions. She knew judges like her should make impartial decisions based purely on the evidence. They were there to advise juries and to help them interpret data and facts, not have intuitions or hunches. Not to interfere with a colleague's work.

'Once in a while,' she said, 'it must be right to trust your guts despite the evidence. I recognise evil when I see it and Stephen Bailey is evil personified.'

And such a contrast to Amelia, whose school prom photograph sat on the Welsh dresser. A picture of promise. Her skimpy, black dress left little to the imagination, but her make-up was subtle and her hair long and flowing. The third in a line of girls, all competent young women in the making, posing along one side of a silver-grey stretch limousine. An equal number of boys lounged on the other side, looking less confident and less comfortable in their hired black-tie gear.

There should be more photographs on the dresser. Graduation, an engagement party, a wedding. Instead, there was a blue and white jug with straggly, wilting sweet peas. Harriet knew how they felt. But no matter. They were there. Harriet had been stunned when Amelia, who knew she was dying, asked her mother to keep fresh flowers on the dresser.

'Nothing fancy. Not expensive. Something simple to remind you of me.'

Did she think they needed flowers to remind them?

'But, of course, we will. Flowers. We will always have flowers. We'll remember our walks down the lane and the day you picked all the daffodils from Magda's front garden for Mothering Sunday.'

Harriet grabbed the newspaper, peered at the grainy picture which leapt off the front page. The beaming nine-month-old in the photo looked like Amelia at the same age with her wispy, fair hair and pink rabbit comforter. Stephen had his arm fixed possessively around Tracey's shoulders. His fringe was swept back and his hair was hanging over his collar. He was smiling at the girls, his white teeth showing. Harriet wasn't fooled. She wouldn't let him care for a dog, let alone children. Tracey was looking away from the camera, distracted, not fully present. Her greasy hair was pulled back in a ponytail and her skin was pale and unhealthy. If she was trying to disguise her anxiety, she wasn't doing it very well.

The lawyer had issued a statement: Tammy had been much loved and mourned. Now the family deserved privacy as they carried on with their lives. The Baileys would be suing the police, the courts, and the judge for wrongful arrest, conviction, and false imprisonment. Not for the money, of course, but so that lessons would be learned and no other parent would have to endure similar suffering.

'And now those two little girls will be dragged, and I mean dragged, from the safety of their grandparents' home to live with an inadequate mother and a devious, cunning father. And not *three* miles – *three* miles from here.'

'They won't remember what happened to Tammy, will they?' said Roger. 'Dinner's in the oven, by the way.'

'I can smell it. You're an angel. Yes, they were babies. Bet you, he'll be back inside by Christmas, and let's hope Jayden and Leanne will still be alive. I hope Sir Godfrey can sleep at night.'

Roger was chopping green beans and cutting chunks of bread. Harriet gave silent thanks for her husband's patience. 'Let's hope that for once you're wrong and Godfrey's right. You don't think you're getting a bit obsessed?'

Asparagus sizzled in butter. The smell of chicken stuffed with Roquefort and wrapped in pancetta drifted across the room. Harriet replaced the sweet peas with roses fresh from the garden, and breathed in the summery perfume of *Amelia*, the aptly named rose they had planted in her memory.

'Maybe,' she said, burrowing her nose in the pink petals, mindful that the anniversary always unsettled her. 'But I can't get the crime scene pictures out of my head. I've seen terrible things but this was worse than anything. Tammy was unrecognisable. She didn't stand a chance.'

After a civilised meal, a bottle of Sancerre, and a cafetière of strong coffee, she kicked off her sandals, put her feet up on the Chesterfield, and watched Roger smiling to himself. He looked smug, and content. If only she could be as satisfied with a pleasant evening and a good meal.

'Early night?'

Harriet was perching on a low brick wall in the car park, waiting for Donna Thomas, the child welfare officer. She could tell from Donna's face she wasn't welcome. Saw the effort she was making to be polite. Heard her say how busy she was and how late for her next appointment.

'I hear you and Bethan have been visiting Tracey,' said Harriet. 'I bet the place was messy and the children were watching a shopping channel.'

'With *respect*, Judge,' said Donna, 'it's not your case and I can't tell you about my home visits. Bethan has no right to tell you anything either. It's confidential. And for the record . . .' she jiggled her car keys, and pressed the zapper, 'watching QVC isn't a culpable offence. If we arrested every parent whose house smelled of piss, we'd need to build a new prison.'

'Is anybody helping Tracey with the children? What about school places? Is Bailey being watched?'

'Look!' Donna threw her bag on the passenger seat. 'On Thursdays, they go to their grandparents. They get spoiled rotten and stay over until their dad collects them on Friday after work. I was there last week when he came in and they leapt all over him, all smiles. I'm only telling you all this because it's not exactly classified information. Believe me, we're all doing our best.'

'What about schools?'

'This is not your job, Judge. I have to go.'

Harriet went back to Chambers and threw herself into preparation for her next trial. A difficult one, but nothing as heart-rending as the Bailey case. She made perfunctory notes on her pad, speedread the papers, and skimmed through others. What about Jayden's school place? Would Tracey be able to fill the form in? Would Donna have enough time to help her? She downloaded the application form from the school website and put it in an envelope. She would drop it in on her way home. See for herself what was going on.

It took a while for Tracey to come to the door. One little girl with pigtails stood beside her, holding a rag doll. Her thumb was firmly fixed in her mouth. Harriet smiled.

'You don't know me, Tracey,' she said. 'I work at the court and. . .'

'And what?' She spat the words out. 'Why can't you lot leave us alone? I've had the vicar poking her nose in, the social worker virtually lives here, and now you.'

Harriet took the envelope from her bag. 'I wanted to help. I've printed the school application form off for Jayden.'

'We've done that online,' said Tracey. 'Stephen's dead good at computers. That's where she is now. She started a bit later than the other children, that's all. We don't need no do-gooders interfering.' The child was pushed back into the hall and the door slammed. Harriet scrunched up the form and stuffed it back in her bag, strode back to her car, and headed off to the school.

'Mrs Parmenter,' said Mrs Marshall, the deputy head, in a voice she usually saved for the neediest parents. 'You're a professional woman. I can't and I won't talk to anybody about our families unless they have the proper authority. Donna and I are in constant touch. All I will tell you is Jayden is fine and everything is under control.'

'But you didn't see the pictures. You don't know what he's like. It only takes a few seconds to injure a child and I might be able. . .'

'You're not able to do anything. I'm well aware of the safeguarding issues and you're not helping. Go back to work. Go home.'

As Harriet was about to respond, they were interrupted by the buzz of the door being opened by the receptionist. It was Donna. She stood stock still. Stared at Harriet. Looked to Mrs Marshall for help.

'Mrs Parmenter was about to leave.' She opened the door and beckoned to Harriet. 'And Ms Thomas, as you see, is making her weekly visit to see Jayden.'

'Yes, I see. I'm sorry to have interrupted you.'

Donna, open-mouthed, watched her through the window as she got back into her car. Harriet wound down the window, took deep breaths. She would sit for a few minutes, make a few calls, and compose herself before returning to the office.

A week later, Harriet was cruising through the town and found herself driving along School Lane. It was like the car had a mind of its own she told Roger later that evening. Like a magnet was drawing her to Swan Meadows. She parked out of sight and well away from the yellow zigzag lines, while she worked out what to do. Did she dare go in again? She got out, walked along the road, and stood watching children chasing around the playground like excited puppies. She closed her eyes and listened to the babble of happy voices, balls bouncing and skipping ropes whirring. When she opened them again, she saw three little girls playing hopscotch, their red jumpers tied around their waists. She was sure she recognised the one with the plaits.

'Jayden!' she called, peering through the wire mesh. 'Jayden! Over here. What are you playing?' The girl turned at the sound of her name. Harriet watched the three linking arms, looking hesitantly at one another. The boldest one steered the others away from the fence towards the climbing frame and the teacher who was on duty. Harriet turned away. She returned to her car and unwrapped a chocolate bar. She nibbled it slowly, wondering whether Donna had understated the case, missed the danger signs, or whether she, Harriet, was losing her mind.

The blaring sirens grew louder. She watched the ambulance stop on the yellow lines. Saw the receptionist run out and punch in numbers to open the gate. Followed the paramedics with her eyes as they ran through the front door with their bulky rucksacks. Where were they going in such a hurry? More sirens. A police car this time.

She sat in her car and fiddled with the rear-view mirror. It was irrational to think it was Jayden. She was safe inside, well away from Stephen. She would wait, for a short while, and see what happened. There could be any number of reasons why an ambulance was needed. A child with a nut allergy, a fall in the gym, a paintbrush in the eye. Please God, just an alarm. Nothing serious. A paramedic came to fetch a wheelchair from the vehicle. A few minutes later, he was pushing the wheelchair and Donna was hurrying along beside him. Donna, holding a tiny hand, inching out from a bundle of blankets strapped into the chair. That wasn't Jayden. It was Leanne. She retched. She'd forgotten Leanne was at nursery. The ambulance door slammed, the sirens screeched and the vehicle left. Then two police officers walked out with a man. It was Bailey. Stephen Bailey.

She turned on the engine and pulled away cautiously. The police car wasn't rushing so she was able to tail it easily. What was she doing? At the hospital, she cursed the car park queue, drove around for several minutes before finding a space, and, ignoring the pay and display signs, ran through the rows of cars into Accident and Emergency.

She couldn't see them in the waiting area. There were parents with children in various states of distress, an old man accompanied by a carer in a magenta uniform, a woman with a polystyrene cup. She would have to be patient. Keep an eye on the exits. She could see a single police car from where she was sitting. She'd be first to know if they left with or without Bailey.

Should she put things in motion to get an emergency protection order? Would Donna have done it already? And where was Tracey? The child needed her mother. For an hour, nobody came or went. She decided to take her chance and make her way to Puffin ward. She'd pretend to be a relative or an official. She took the stairs two at a time, not bothering to wait for the lift. As she rounded the corner, she recognised Donna's back vanishing into the ward and the door being closed. She took five or six breaths to steady herself. This was Amelia's ward. She pressed the intercom buzzer.

'I'm a lawyer. I'm with the Bailey case,' she said to the disembodied voice. It was obvious which room Leanne was in as a uniformed police officer was guarding the door. 'I'm a lawyer. What's the state of play?'

The officer had the look of a student about him. He exuded nervousness. No match for a seasoned judge. 'Mr Bailey's in the relatives' room with my colleagues if you want to see him. He's beside himself. Must be terrible when it's your kid. Don't know why he wants a solicitor. He's not under arrest or anything '

'Not yet,' said Harriet. 'And the child?'

'They're waiting for scan results. Doc's with her now. She collapsed at school and they were worried it was meningitis. They took her clothes off to cool her down and found the bruises. That's why we were called. And social services.'

Make all the excuses you like, thought Harriet. Blame the economy, the rich, the government, or the education system. Nothing justified battering a child. Her reverie was disturbed by raised voices and doors banging.

'My daughter's in there and nobody is going to stop me seeing her. You have no fucking right to stop me. What the hell has the bitch done now?'

The voice faltered and came to a halt. Stephen Bailey stood outside the relatives' room, sobbing. He slumped into the red, plastic chair in the corridor. Stephen Bailey. Sobbing. Had he really said 'What's the bitch done now?'

Another Friday night. Another meal around the marble island. Sea bass, broad beans, chorizo, and wild rice. Amelia's photo, forever speaking of unfulfilled promise, an orange gerbera sitting in a terracotta pot.

'I don't know if it's worse to be in the right or the wrong.'

Roger raised his eyebrows. 'I was right to be sceptical but wrong in every other way. I've lost all confidence. In myself, the law, women. How could any mother do that?'

'Well, if it's any consolation, Sir Godfrey was wrong, too.'

'Hah! But not completely. He wasn't taken in. Why did we all blame Stephen Bailey? The police were adamant it was him and Tracey must have been questioned the first time around.'

'Well, Stephen drew all the attention to himself, didn't he? He'd been told it might be a serious bout of post-natal depression. Decided the girls needed their mother more than him. He must have loved them very much.'

'And he must have been going through hell worrying about Jayden and Leanne, especially when he was in prison or working late.'

'As he was on that Monday night. Anyway, the girls will be fine and Tracey is where she belongs. Maybe badgering the poor social worker was worth it.'

'Don't think so. I was completely out of order and I've told her as much. I sent her a case of Sauvignon. Do you think that counts as bribery? To add to my many offences. But that little girl got under my skin. And she affected Bethan, as well. It wasn't only me. Even she was talking about how hard it is to believe in a loving God when there's this much cruelty in the world but I should have known better.'

'Which is why, when the case comes to court, you will maintain total silence. Keep your opinions to yourself.'

Harriet moved her fish around her plate. Picked up her wine glass.

'I'll do more than that, Roger. 'I could have put myself into very deep water. I've had very embarrassing conversations with the powers that be. Unprofessional behaviour, lack of judgment. And it's all true. What would you say if I retired a year early?'

'Of course, my love, if that's what you've decided. We don't need the money. But what would you do all day? You're a right pain when you're bored.'

'Not sure yet. Every time I see Amelia's flowers, I think about the happy life she had, even if it was only for nineteen years, and the rotten time other kids have. I'll find ways to improve things. Charity work. Lobbying the government? Setting up trust funds for children like Jayden and Leanne.'

Roger opened a new bottle. Refilled their glasses.

'I'll drink to that,' he said.

21. Nicki's Story

Nicki had been attracted by his rippling muscles and strawberry blond hair, when she and Leah happened upon the crew leaving the boathouse.

'Who's the hunk in the blue lycra?' she'd asked.

'Which one? They're all wearing blue lycra.'

'The one with the hair.'

'Oh, Dave. He's in my tutor group. Reading Classics. Nice guy. Bit competitive.'

'Nice guy? He's unbelievable. Let's bump into him and you can introduce me.'

It was ten years since she'd 'bumped into' David. Ten years since she'd persuaded Leah to accompany her to the boathouse every morning for a week.

'Don't want to be taken for a mad stalker. Safety in numbers and all that.'

Nicki had finally gained his attention and they'd had a brief conversation or two. Leah stopped tagging along but Nicki went morning after morning, even when it was dark and cold. Did he appreciate what a labour of love that was for a night owl, she asked him on the day his crew lost the boat race? He was drowning his sorrows and she was cashing in on his vulnerability and taking her chance.

'You may not have won a gold medal but you can have me any time you like,' she ventured, emboldened by one too many beers. Hard to believe how happy they'd been then, and how unhappy they'd become over the last few weeks. First, months where nothing happened, then Mr

Wilson and his damning report, David's unequivocal rejection of a sperm donor, and Mr White Teeth's final nail in the coffin.

But then they had a plan and a spreadsheet, and she and David were on the same side again. They had made a decision. The way forward was adoption.

It had been a long journey, and the adoption panel loomed like a medieval ordeal. There had been a tricky moment when David had joked with the social worker he would have to bribe a friend to write a positive reference. They'd had a major row about that.

'Don't say anything flippant,' warned Nicki. 'Don't make jokes or be facetious or sarcastic.'

'What me? You mean, don't say we're sending our kids down the mines once they're seven. Or that we plan to leave them outside *The Dog and Duck* with a bag of crisps every Friday night?'

'That's exactly what I mean. Just don't.'

Finally, the gruelling process was over and the news was good. They were approved as prospective adoptive parents. It was just a matter of time before a tiny human being made his or her way into their lives. What could possibly go wrong now?

The twins, Tyler and Alfie, were a few weeks old when David and Nicki first saw them. Non-identical, underweight brothers born to a teenage mother after a one-night stand. She didn't know the father's name, had no supportive relationships, no job, and was living in a bed and breakfast. She had decided adoption would give the boys a better chance.

'She's a decent kid, despite all she's been through,' said Josie. 'Wants the best for them. She's making a real sacrifice for all the right reasons. Her parents can't or won't help out and have washed their hands of her and the boys. Won't even see them.'

Nicki felt like the child snatcher from *Chitty Chitty Bang Bang*. This girl's crisis was her and David's salvation. Their joy was at the expense of a young mother and her unbending parents. It was like hoping somebody else would die so you could have his kidney. David was more sanguine.

'We're going to do what she wants. Give the boys a bright future. She's thought everything through and made the right decision.'

They painted the nursery, assembled cots and regularly visited the foster home, getting to know the babies.

'I'm sure Tyler is smiling at me,' David said after their third visit.

'And Alfie has such a strong grip, doesn't he? I think he turns his head when he hears my voice.'

'They're going to love the musical mobiles.'

'Why does it all take so long?'

When Josie asked to visit them four days before Christmas, they assumed she was coming to finalise the details. Shame they weren't going to have them in time for Christmas but a few more days didn't matter As soon as they were settled in the living room, coffee pot on the table between them, she launched in.

'There's no easy way to say this. I won't mess around. I'm so sorry to have to tell you that Tyler died in the night.'

Nicki's eyes widened. David shuffled around on the sofa.

'But he can't have,' said David. 'We were with him yesterday. He smiled at me.'

'They're conducting a post-mortem this morning and Alfie's having tests in case there's a genetic problem. I can't tell you how sorry I am.'

'What will we do with all the Christmas presents?' said Nicki.

'What will Alfie do without Tyler?' What would *they* do without him?

They struggled through Christmas, refusing all offers of hospitality, company, or visits. They left the presents under the tree and swept the festive food back into the larder and fridge. They wept with the foster carers on Christmas Eve as they took turns hugging Alfie, and, even more, when they reached home. The coroner's report was delayed because of the holiday and it would be an interim one. There would have to be an inquest. Nobody could say how long it would take or when Alfie would be theirs.

'I'm afraid there's good and bad news,' said Josie, as she sat in their living room again. The only evidence of the tree was the needles lying along the skirting board and sticking into the carpet. Forlorn remnants of the holiday were visible – a half-burnt candle and a couple of escapee cards still hiding behind the curtain.

'Turns out Tyler had a rare, genetic heart condition which nobody could have foreseen. But Alfie is fit and healthy as far as they can tell. His scans all look fine.'

Nicki sighed. Breathed deeply. 'Thank goodness! We'll watch him like a hawk. We'll get one of those things you can put on his ankle. A smart sock I think it's called.'

'We'll make sure he gets regular checks with every

medic we can find,' said David. 'He may not have his brother but he'll have us.'

Josie sighed, sipped from her mug and read her notes again. There were tears in her eyes when she spoke.

'I'm afraid it's not that simple. Alfie's birth mother has changed her mind. She wants to keep him. Losing Tyler has made her think again and her parents have come around, in every sense, and offered them both a home. The minute they saw him, they were converted.'

Three months later, Nicki and David found themselves sitting in Josie's temporary, demountable office with its slippery, grey armchairs. A jar of instant coffee and an open packet of tea bags sat on a side table by an electric kettle with chunky, mismatched mugs and broken digestives. Josie rushed in, files bulging from her tote bag, hair escaping from its velvet scrunchie.

'Sorry to keep you waiting,' she said, as she sat down. 'It's been a mad day.'

There was no time for chat beyond mere pleasantries. Josie didn't mince words. She didn't have time.

'When you said you didn't want to come to another adoption day, I went back to the drawing board.'

'It was awful. I wanted to be the new Dr Barnardo and take them all home.'

'And going through all those files was like searching for a used car on eBay,' said David. 'Choosing one child meant rejecting several others.'

'And we'd struggled to come to terms with losing the twins.'

Josie nodded. 'Well, I have good vibes about this little girl. She's nine months old and she's available for immediate adoption. The court has ruled the mother is unable to provide a safe environment for her and her father's serving time for a violent offence. Not against the baby though. She's absolutely fine.'

She placed a photo album on the table. 'I'll come back in a while and see what you think. She has your hair colouring, David, and her name is Zöe.'

' Zöe? She's called Zöe? I don't believe it.'

Josie looked at him, raised her eyebrows.

'What's wrong with Zöe?' Nicki asked. 'I quite like it.'

'Nothing's wrong with it. It's like a sign.'

David had never expressed a single religious or spiritual idea in all the time she had known him. Had scoffed at her for suggesting prayer might be the answer. Where was this coming from?

'A sign? Like how? You haven't seen her photo yet.'

'I have a deadly condition called azoospermia. It means *life is not possible* or words to that effect. Zöe means life. Anyone with a smattering of Classics knows that. It's like she's a gift. She's making up for everything we've lost.'

'I love her already,' said Nicki, opening the album.

On Zöe's second birthday, the phone rang.

'Hi, there, Nicki. This is Josie.'

'Josie?'

'From the Adoption Service. You can't have forgotten me?'

'Oh no, of course not. How are you?' *and why on earth are you ringing? She's ours. We signed the papers. You're not having her back.* Nicki knew her reaction was irrational but after all they'd been through, you never knew.

'How's Zöe?'

'Smothered in yellow icing at the minute.' *Is that the wrong thing to say?* As if on cue, Zöe flung her Peter Rabbit bowl across the room, laughed when she saw the cake flying everywhere and rubbed the icing in her curly hair.

'We had no idea it would be this wonderful,' said Nicki. 'She's a total delight.'

'That's marvellous. I wondered if I could visit you and David one day next week?'

'Yes. I guess so. When? Why?'

'Nothing to worry about. I'd rather talk face to face.'

'You should have said no,' said David when Zöe was having a nap and they were clearing up the mess.

'How could I? Anyway, Zöe's ours. Maybe she likes to check in now and again.'

'We'd better have a spring clean. Make sure we have plenty of children's books on view.' As she spoke, she was rearranging the photos of Zöe in the paddling pool, Zöe on David's shoulders, Zöe in the snow. Would Josie notice the cobwebs behind the TV? Why was she feeling defensive? The adoption had been finalised. Nobody could take their daughter away from them now.

Josie's bag was still overflowing, her hair still trying to escape from its scrunchie. She made all the right noises about the photos and the books, wolfed down the homemade biscuits, and sat on the floor with Zöe who was putting her doll to bed in its crib.

'I expect you're wondering why I'm here.' Nicki and David nodded.

' Zöe's doing well, isn't she?' They nodded again.

'We were wondering whether you're ready to adopt a second child.'

'No,' said David. 'Yes,' said Nicki.

'Well, I wasn't expecting that,' said David. 'It's a bit of a shock. Aren't we meant to wait three years?'

'Ye-es,' said Josie.

'So, what aren't you saying?'

' Zöe's birth mother is expecting another baby. In the summer. A boy. The baby will be taken away from her at birth.'

'But, what, how?'

'Her situation hasn't changed and we believe the baby will be at risk. We try to keep siblings together where we can, and the three-year rule doesn't apply in that case. Could you cope with another child?'

Nicki and David looked at one another. Said nothing.

'At the drop of a hat, you're offering us two for the price of one.'

'Hardly the drop of a hat, David. You've been through a rigorous process and there would be another interview to check you haven't had a personality transplant or grown two heads in the last few months.'

'But what you're saying is, he's ours if we want him,' said Nicki looking out at the double swing they'd installed for Zöe's birthday.

'You don't have to decide immediately, but we'll need to make plans for him one way or another. And, there's one more thing. He doesn't have the same father.'

'Well, obviously,' said David. 'Presumably, the first one's still in prison.'

'Yeah. But the thing is, there were two brothers and the birth mother can't say which one is the father.'

'Does it matter?' asked Nicki.

'Well, no. But the brothers are black.'

Nicki lay in bed. The bright green figures on her phone told her it was 04:20.

'You awake?' she said, knowing the answer. David grunted.

'How are you?'

'Excited. Bemused. Worried. Tired. And you?'

'All of the above,' said Nicki. 'And scared about the multicultural thing. Is it important?'

'Well. It doesn't have to be. Everyone will know we're not his genetic parents and he'll be different from Zöe, but who cares? It's England for goodness' sake. Not Alabama.'

'But I'm worried we're saying that because we think we should. They say everybody has racist tendencies. What if we can't love him because he's different?'

'I'm more worried about something going wrong,' said David. 'Not the colour of his skin. He's not born yet. What if he dies?'

Davidwas still buttering his toast the next morning when Nicki, unable to contain herself, rushed into the kitchen, laptop under her arm, Zöe toddling behind her.

'I want the baby, David. I know we're tired and it's earlier than we planned and he'll be different but. . .'

'You do? Thank God!' he said softly. 'Me, too.'

'And this time,' said Nicki when she had strapped Zöe into the high chair and given her cereal and a spoon, 'We get to choose the name.' She opened her laptop and showed him her list.

'I was thinking. Zöe means life and she was our first gift. This baby will be our second, surprise gift. I've found 405 boys' names which mean gift. Yes, honestly! I've deleted the ones I can't pronounce.'

'That's a relief.' David picked up his toast with one hand and scrolled down the list with the other.

'Derrick? I don't think so. Theodore? pretentious. Zebediah? You *are* joking? Let's talk about it properly tonight but, for now I like Jonathan and Matthew. Either is fine by me.'

When Josie rang to say the baby had been born and his birth mother had called him Nathan, they were overjoyed.

'Don't say it,' said Nicki. 'It's another sign.'

'Well, it is spooky. But it means we can honour her choice and change his name to make him our own.'

' Zöe and Jonathan. Our double gifts.'

Zöe was alternately bored by the baby and besotted with him.

'Baby go,' she would say when she had had enough, or 'Zo cuddle baby' if she thought she was missing out.

'All perfectly normal,' said Josie, as she watched Zöe clinging to Nicki's legs. 'You look very settled there, David, giving Jonathan his bottle. Gazing into each other's eyes. You're a picture of contentment.'

Nicki smiled as David responded.

'Despite all the disappointments and the uncertainty and angst, I wouldn't swap these two for anything. We're enjoying being like other parents: exhausted, no energy, no money, and sleep-deprived. We're a complete family and we couldn't be happier.'

On Jonathan's second birthday, the phone rang.

'Hi, there, Nicki. It's me. Josie.'

22. *The Boxing Day Shout*

You'd think losing a son was hard enough Losing your husband as well was cruel beyond belief. Who could go through a double bereavement and still stand? Louise had no choice but to get up every morning for the sake of her two daughters. She was more courageous than I knew how to be.

Yesterday, I was Paul's wife. Today, I am his widow. Simple as that. But I've been here before. I used to have three children. And now there are two.

You might think you understand what it's like for me. Maybe people in uniform have stood on your doorstep and you knew what was coming before they opened their mouths. Maybe you, too, have wondered when the drama would be over and you'd get on with real life again. And then, maybe it hit you as it did me. This *is* real life now. But don't think you understand what I'm going through, for you're not me, and Paul wasn't your husband. You're not me, and Tom wasn't your son.

Tom died from a brain tumour. Paul was in the army for most of his working life so we'd written and re-written our wills many times. Death was always hovering and hiding like an unwelcome guest so you'd think I'd have been better prepared this time around. I knew there was a sealed envelope locked away in a cabinet somewhere with my name on it, to be opened in the event of death. It was the hardest thing about being a chaplain, Paul said, helping raw recruits write those 'Dear Mum' letters before their first tour, and knowing if it happened to you, the envelope would be winging its way by messenger to your loved ones.

Every time the doorbell or the phone rang early in the morning or late at night, I would steel myself to hear the calm, well-rehearsed, slightly wary voice which would tell me Paul had died or been seriously injured. There were times we had no communication at all when they had to hand their mobiles in for security. But Paul survived the landmines, the snipers, the terrorist attacks, and the sunstroke, frostbite, desert winds, and drought. Our *marriage* survived despite the months of separation and the awkward coming together every time he was on leave. Kate and Jo grew up. Barely a scar to show they were military *and* clergy kids.

'A double burden,' complained Jo.

'A double *bonus*,' Tom used to say, with a wisdom beyond his years. 'Dad can do his caring, sharing, praying stuff and still get a proper salary and pension. And we can bask in the reflected glory of his holiness and courage.' There was more bravado in his words than he let on. Of course, he worried about Paul as much as I did. Just didn't want anyone to know.

Paul's a vicar in a seaside town now. He *was* a vicar in a seaside town. We've been here for two years. Long enough to know the pitfalls but not long enough for the Archdeacon to be muttering about 'giving us a new challenge.' We didn't want a challenge. We wanted to be settled and together.

I wasn't the least bit concerned when Paul joined the lifeboat crew. Quite the opposite. It gave him male company and fulfilled his need to save people and, now and again, animals. The crews welcomed him with open arms. Paul was a natural, they said. He came back from successful shouts proud as punch. The salty seaweed smell permeated every room. You'll be wondering why, when his pager went off in the early hours of Boxing Day morning, I did nothing more than pull the duvet up and around my neck. You're wondering why I didn't register the rain hammering on the windows, or why it didn't occur to me that a call-out at two a.m. was unlikely to be an injured dog. You're maybe wondering whether I am deaf and blind and missed the lightning and thunder altogether.

I wonder, too. Truth to tell, we stayed up late on Christmas night watching rubbish T.V. with the girls. We'd opened all the presents and started on the bottles donated by grateful parishioners. Paul knew he was on call so all the more for me. We must have dragged ourselves to bed long after midnight. By then, I was three sheets to the wind, pardon the tasteless pun.

When I woke to the light filtering through the curtains, the clock said nine-twenty. Paul must be downstairs making the tea. Then the doorbell rang. I hunkered down, waiting for the sound of his footsteps. When the bell rang again, it was obvious he wasn't within earshot. Retrieving my dressing gown from the floor, I stumbled downstairs, thinking things a vicar's wife should definitely *not* be thinking.

Before I'd reached the door and while I fumbled with the doorknob, I glimpsed the two bulky blue and yellow figures. You'll think I'm completely dense, but Paul used to forget his key sometimes and often brought a mate back for a brew. Then as soon as I saw them, I knew. My eyes told me what the night had been like. Water was streaming down towards the quay, an ancient beech tree had come down in the garden opposite, half blocking the lane, and two men in knee-high fishing trousers were striding down the pavement, one with a labradoodle in his arms. My heart told me the rest.

The sky was disconcertingly blue, white clouds scudding along like children out to play. They were moving on to ruin somebody else's life, leaving our town and all the towns along our coast to pick up the pieces.

'I'm sorry, Lou,' said Skip, his voice breaking. 'Can we come in?'

I could barely move, fiddled with my dressing gown cord, pulling it tight, twisting it between my fingers. I wanted to scream but no words would come. That familiar smell of seaweed and tangy salt water was no longer attractive but invasive, repellent.

The commotion had disturbed the girls who followed me downstairs. They were equally dishevelled, pulling dressing gowns around them. Kate grabbed hold of me to stop me from crumpling to the floor. Jo snatched at a chair and positioned it behind me.

'It's Dad,' I said, stating the obvious.

I looked at the men for confirmation. The word had not been spoken yet. They nodded.

'He fell in. Trying to jump onto the other boat. Slipped down between the two.' They spoke in broken sentences, taking turns to get the story out.

'A massive gust of wind turned the boat at the last minute. The waves were the size of a house, Lou. We couldn't do anything.'

Skip and Ken, grown men, were in tears. I wanted to say if we all sat down calmly and had a cup of tea, we could find a solution. It couldn't be as bad as all that. The kind of thing I used to say when one of the children was upset over a minor crisis. Until Tom got a brain tumour and that evil intruder was worse than anything we could imagine.

Kate and Jo stood there, clutching one another, as Skip and Ken dripped water all over the hall floor. Lucky there's no carpet, I found myself thinking.

'We've, we've recovered his body,' said Ken as if that were a consolation. Which, I suppose it was. At least we had one to bury. He could keep Tom company.

'Paul volunteered to jump, didn't he?'

They looked uneasily at each other.

'Yes. He was sure he could do it. Said we should concentrate on getting a guy with a broken leg onto the lifeboat.'

'If we could have had a helicopter. . .but there was no way it could fly in this. And if we'd turned back and left them. . .' He couldn't complete the sentence. We all knew the other guy would have died. Instead, it was Paul.

'As he was waiting to jump, Paul turned around, just for a second, and shouted, "Tell Lou and the girls I love them". And then he was gone. The bravest thing I've ever seen.'

I don't know whether Skip had made that up to make me feel better, but it's the kind of thing Paul would have said so I chose to believe him. Jo let out a strangled cry. Tears streamed down Kate's face. The men went off to tell the tale to their own families.

We have had many horrible Boxing Days. When Paul was serving abroad, I made the best of it for the children's sake. When he was home on leave, every minute of fun took us closer to the moment he'd go again. The first Christmas after Tom died was unspeakable. It was hard to imagine celebrating Christmas ever again. There was always going to be a Tom-shaped hole. Now Paul will be missing too and we will re-live this Boxing Day over and over and over again.

We shall have to move. Perhaps we'll go back to Swannery. We still have friends there. We kept up with Roger and Harriet. They knew exactly what it was like to lose a child and the girls loved school there. Except, that's where Tom died so I don't know. We'll survive. We always do, but don't tell me it was the same for you and you know what I'm feeling because you're not me and Paul wasn't your husband. Yesterday I was Paul's wife. Today, I'm his widow. Simple as that.

23. *The Chocolate Cake*

I loved the fairs and fetes which were such an integral part of village life: the amateurish sideshows, second-hand bookstalls and country dancing, the school recorder group's enthusiastic performance of Frère Jacques and the hot dog stalls smelling of onions and mustard. Most of all, I loved the exhibitions, the art, flowers and marmalade, the misshapen vegetables and the Cygnets' self-portraits which only a mother could love. Who would have thought ours would have produced such drama, and that Audrey would save the day.

'You bitch,' Bernard Wainwright screeched from the other side of the marquee.

'Second prize. Second prize? A blue rosette? Is that all I'm worth? Roger Parmenter's only won because he's the churchwarden. I can't believe you've given him first prize. Again.'

Audrey, this year's vice president, watched him pick up the plate on which his second-class, triple-layer chocolate gateau was resting precariously. She realized with horror he was about to hurl it at her friend, Fiona, judge of the bakery section.

'No!' she shouted, but it was too late. She saw Fiona's arms come up in defence and then watched as she fell onto a chair underneath a brown goo, the remains of Bernard's precious offering. The frosted icing had already been struggling in the airless tent and now formed marbled streaks down her cheeks. There were lumps of cake in her hair and crumbs across her bright yellow, silk blouse. A couple of teenagers whooped with delight, and there were stifled groans of disbelief from those who had witnessed this unbelievable performance.

'Somebody *do* something,' yelled Audrey.

But she was the one in charge. She was the person who had to do something to sort out this unholy mess. She had agreed to stand as vice president because she owed the vicar a favour. It was Bethan who had helped Audrey get a job and find a flat, and persuaded her not to move away from everything and everyone she knew. Wait and see what Henry does, Bethan had said. Sometimes, bullies get bored and move on. Especially if their victims stand up to them.

She should have known it took stronger women than her to corral the warring personalities in the parochial confines of the annual fair. There were only a few more hours to go before she could relax. She wouldn't have to wake in a cold sweat thinking about classes and medals tonight. It had been exhausting herding the judges around all morning. Waiting for them to make decisions and stick with them, watching them attach rosettes on the prize-winning exhibits and standing back for one last look, aware of the competitors peeping through the tent flaps, desperate to see if they'd won.

She'd taken a deep breath, inhaling the scent of sweet peas, roses and freesias, vinegary pickled onions, and yeasty ginger beer. Then she'd untied the strings holding the flaps together and stood back. Pushchairs clanged against wheelchairs, shopping bags and toddlers got in the way of adult legs and arms. Any minute now, somebody's prize work of art was going to be knocked over and trampled on. She hadn't expected Bernard to throw one at a judge.

Bernard Wainwright was tall and spindly with a tidy moustache and frameless glasses which meant you could never be sure he was wearing them until you got close. He had been a churchwarden and a magistrate, a thoroughly unlikely person to engage in a deliberate act of violence. His wife's name appeared on the silver rose bowl more times than any other person, but she'd died three years ago.

His first attempt in the show before last had been a Victoria sponge with a homemade jam filling. It hadn't warranted even a *highly commended.* When he was awarded a blue rosette last year, he was ecstatic. This year, Audrey knew he'd pinned his hopes on first prize, perhaps best in the section. Organic flour, best Cornish butter, free-range eggs. Nothing was left to chance.

Mrs Bowman, Fiona to her few, chosen friends, was Bernard's antithesis. While he was thin and insubstantial, every bone in his face visible, his hair grey and wispy, she was bordering on plump with thick, long hair piled on her head. She had been the senior judge in the baking section for fifteen years and head of domestic science at the comprehensive school for longer. There she had intimidated quivering teenagers. Now she was bringing her single-minded style to bear on a variety of village societies, not least the Swannery Country Fair Committee.

Audrey had watched Mr Wainwright push his way into the tent, down the side aisles, past the elderflower cordial, onion sets and coconut flapjacks. She knew he'd be disgruntled but she hadn't expected this. Those committee members who were still capable of rushing without the aid of sticks sped to the scene. Magda grabbed Fiona's elbow and rearranged her body in the regulation village hall chair she had landed in. She was struggling to speak. Audrey steered Wainwright away, clutching his arm like a police officer about to snap on the handcuffs. There hadn't been so much excitement since 1987 when the Bailey boys had managed to turn the fire engine hoses on, soaking the mayor and his obese, heavily bejewelled consort.

'Let's get you a nice cup of tea,' said Magda to her friend. 'Take a deep breath and we'll have you right as rain. I'm sure the stain will come out if you soak it overnight.'

Unlikely, thought Audrey.

'How about a cuppa,' she said to Mr Wainwright. 'It's not worth getting wound up about. It's only a village fair.'

Both parties protested, but green cups and saucers appeared out of nowhere and were thrust into reluctant hands. Nobody was brave or stupid enough to offer cake. Fiona Bowman slammed her cup and saucer down on the table, sloshing the tea all over the white, paper tablecloth. She turned her head at an uncomfortable angle to view the yellow silk shoulder and burst into tears. The painters and potters muttered while the knitters pretended to be busy. The victorious Mr Parmenter and his usually assertive wife were uncomfortable. Anybody could see that. This wasn't how Audrey wanted the day to end. She could see the headline on the front page of the Recorder: Country Fair Chocolate Gate.

Where was the vicar when you needed her? Anyone who could negotiate a change of hymn books and keep all factions singing could manage a case of biased judging if such it was. In her absence, Audrey would have to cope as best she could.

'Magda, would you escort Fiona to the president's table, please? Bill, would you accompany Mr Wainwright.' She sounded more confident than she felt. She had no idea what would happen when they all arrived there. She had no plan or strategy but it bought her time. When she was trying to escape from Henry Bethan had told her to believe in herself and to take one step at a time. The same could apply now. If she could handle Henry, she could manage Bernard and Fiona.

'Now I can see you're both very upset,' she began when they were both seated, sipping their tea. 'But you're both grown-up people and you're both. . .' she hesitated 'Very good people.' Bill and Magda exchanged glances and raised eyebrows. 'So, we're going to sort this out calmly.'

Where had this new woman sprung from? This was Audrey, the wimpy spectre scared of her own shadow. Somehow, she'd managed to flummox Fiona and quieten Bernard in one easy move. Dear old Bernard's eyes were down, his shoulders hunched, bowed with shame.

'This isn't about coming second, is it Bernard?'

Bernard shook his head, took a blue and white checked hankie out of his trouser pocket, and blew his nose noisily.

'It's about Pru, isn't it?'

He nodded, took off his invisible glasses, and wiped his eyes.

'I didn't want to let her down. She was always winning prizes. I wanted to make her proud.'

'You've made everybody proud,' said Audrey. 'You could hardly boil an egg and make a cheese sandwich before. Now here you are making raspberry jam, baking cakes, and icing them like a professional.'

'It was a very good cake,' said Mrs Bowman. 'Very good indeed.'

Bernard raised his eyes, pursed his lips. Didn't ask the obvious question.

'The middle layer wasn't evenly baked. That's why it didn't come first. Everything else was perfect.'

'And you, Fiona. Retirement not all it's cracked up to be?'

Word was that her friend had been eased out of her job by the new generation of staff, who were young enough to be her grandsons. Marcus, the deputy head, for example. He really didn't like Fiona. Not since she'd made veiled comments about his friend Damian and how odd that they lived at the same address. Unreconstructed. That's what they'd called her. You couldn't harbour views like that and keep your job. Not anymore.

Bernard waited. Magda took a couple of steps back and moved away, wondering whether the committee's insurance policy would cover what was likely to happen next. Had Audrey gone mad?

'Well, I, no, I don't think so.'

'I have a proposal to make,' said Audrey. The voice sounded like somebody else's, quiet yet commanding.

'Bethan tells me several men in the village have been left on their own and are a bit lost in the kitchen. Struggling to cope.'

Nobody said a word.

'They need somebody competent and skilled to bring them together. A good teacher, a recently retired one, maybe, to teach them how to cook for themselves.'

'Well,' said Fiona.

'They also need a male role model. A man who will encourage them to come, and persuade them cooking is for men as well as women, and it's never too late to learn. After all, many of the best chefs are men and your chocolate cake, Bernard, is to die for.'

'It would be if it was still on the plate,' said Fiona, the hint of a smile playing on her lips. 'I suppose I could think about it. If it would help the vicar.'

'And I suppose I might be able to talk one or two of them into coming. Might come myself if I'm free. Sorry I called you a bitch, Fiona. Sorry about your blouse. And your hair.'

'Sorry, you didn't win, Bernard. Maybe next year.'

24. The Merlot and the Blackcurrant Juice

Like domestic violence, addictions know no boundaries. Drugs, pornography, food and drink can take over and destroy lives. Grief provides a ripe and fertile ground for corruption and self-destruction. Verity and Jack's story has a happy ending. Many do not.

'No. Stop! Don't do it.'

How many times have I castigated myself with those words since Jack left for his latest tour of duty? More than my four-year-old daughter could count on her fingers. Sometimes, I thought it from the safety of the bedroom. Sometimes, I whispered it mopping the kitchen floor. Or, forgetting Eloise was in earshot, I shouted out loud. 'No. Stop. Don't do it.'

'But Mummy, I'm not doing anything,' she would say. Then I would smother her with kisses, consumed with guilt.

'Stupid Mummy,' I would laugh. 'It's fine. You're my best girl. You haven't done anything wrong.'

'Maria-at-nursery says it's rude to call people stupid,' she says, once she has the upper hand. And whatever Maria-at-nursery, who must be almost twenty, says is true.

Eloise turns her attention to her dolls, who are never allowed to call anybody stupid. Today, they are Parker and Kayleigh, don't ask why. Whether they will grow up to hide bottles in the laundry basket, nobody knows. Eloise talks non-stop as she pushes them around the garden, struggling to get the wheels over the uneven paving. There's no budget to fix the paths because they're doing away with army housing, but we don't mind. It's good to live close to others in the same situation. Four more sleeps until Jack comes home.

'Sophie's auntie has given her a doll's house,' says Eloise as I plod through the tasks, emptying bins, and sorting laundry. 'But she has to share it with Mia. Can I have a doll's house when Daddy comes home?'

She may only be four years old but she can play the system.

'We'll see.' I pick up the carrots and the peeler. Maria-at-nursery says vegetables are good for you so Eloise eats them without complaint. Parker and Kayleigh always eat their vegetables. Tonight, Daisy is coming to babysit while I go to choir practice. We've met every Tuesday evening since Gareth Malone launched the first Military Wives Choir. Gareth came once, but now we have Damian who is almost as musical but not as charismatic. How could he be? He's a maths teacher. We meet in the community hall on the base and, thank God, we all get a free drink in the interval.

I've been like this for more than a year now but it will pass. There's nothing wrong with me. All the wives like a drink in the evenings. Makes the hours pass more quickly. I'm not going to be defined by what I eat and drink, or how I cope with my sorrow. If you haven't lost a child, you have no right to judge. I *am* putting on weight but that's because it's easier to eat junk food than cook healthy meals, and my skin is dry because I'm out in all weathers walking to school. True, my sleep is erratic and I often wake up more tired than when I go to bed but so would you if you had to sleep on your own for weeks on end. I bet I'm not the only parent who rushes home at nine in the morning to steal the first drink of the day. They probably fail to turn up for meetings sometimes. Maybe their excuses are getting increasingly unconvincing. I am rarely there so there's no way of knowing.

Yet I am not in total denial. Maria-at-nursery would disapprove. I have wondered, researched online, and watched the occasional documentary. And, yes, when I force myself to be honest, I know it's not normal to squirrel bottles away in the Christmas decorations box, and I'm ashamed to admit I spend my child benefit on red wine. But it won't be like that forever. When he comes home, it will be fine. Jack is due back soon for a month's leave. Eloise is so excited she can't contain herself. She crosses the date off the calendar with a red felt tip every morning.

'Three more sleeps before Daddy comes home. Aren't you excited, Mummy? I'm so excited, I can't sit still. Maria-at-nursery says I've got ants in my pants. It doesn't mean you have real ants, though.'

'Of course, I am, my lovely. I'm so excited I could burst. Won't Daddy be surprised to see how clever you are at counting and writing your name?'

'That's what Maria-at-nursery said,' she confides.

She is safely in bed, curled up like a foetus under the fairy duvet cover. That's when my anxiety surfaces. I am like a chicken who has spent all day pretending not to be scared of the fox. I force myself to do essential chores, fill in the permission form for the water park trip and fix tomorrow's packed lunch, then race to the cupboard under the sink, another place nobody else goes.

Here I am, then, me, the TV, and the Merlot. I tell myself it can't be serious if a bottle of red, or two, can do the trick. I resist the spirits real alcoholics crave. I'll be fine when Jack is home. I won't have time to keep thinking about Ben; might be able to banish the image of his lifeless little body in his white velvet sleepsuit, those blue and silver penguins marching up and down, round and round. I can't be a responsible adult on the school trip. I checked the website and they do have penguins. The tears come, as they always do at this time. How can you love a person this much when you only knew them for three short days?

We should have been satisfied, shouldn't we, to have a perfect, healthy daughter waiting for us at home. The hospital staff treated us as though Ben was the only child in the world and we were the first parents to go through this hell. The chaplain didn't insult us with platitudes or promises of life with the angels. Nobody could have done more but nobody could bring Ben back. It was no consolation being told we would be able to have another healthy baby. We didn't want another baby. We wanted Ben.

Two more sleeps until Jack comes home. The hiding places are secure, I hope. He's unlikely to count leftover Christmas crackers or check the disinfectant supply. I have a foolproof strategy for weekdays. He can take Eloise to Cygnets. He'll chat with other parents, go and buy a paper. And after a few relaxing days, and with subtle encouragement, he'll want to get back to the gym. I'll have time for a drink before he gets back and then I'll be fine until evening. Jack always does bath time when he's home, making up for lost time, so I can grab a glass in the utility room while I am sorting the washing. Must buy more peppermints and syphon the wine into blackcurrant bottles.

Who am I trying to kid? He is no fool. He will smell my breath, notice that I am twitchy and irritable and lose my temper at the drop of a hat. He'll want to catch up with friends, and we can't turn down all the invitations. At least, they'll provide plenty of wine. And, though you may not believe me, I hate deceiving him. I love him. The problem is if I don't drink, I can't cope. There, I've said it. I can't cope. Maybe I am an alcoholic after all.

One more sleep until Daddy comes home. How can I hide what I have become from the man who knows every inch of me? Why am I plotting to prevent my husband from seeing me as I am? The beds are changed, the house is cleaned to within an inch of its life, and balloons of varying shapes and sizes drift in the breeze. I've had my hair cut and bought an expensive lipstick called, can you believe it, *sensual rose*. I couldn't feel less sensual if I tried. Eloise's glittery, welcome home card is on the mantelpiece. Everything is in its proper place. All should be right with the world. But it isn't.

Maria says it's a special occasion and Eloise can have the day off despite Sophie's protestations she won't have anybody to play with. Even Mrs Marshall is excited, says Eloise, and she's a very important person with her own office so who am I to contradict? We leave early, Eloise pushing Kayleigh and Parker. We chat about homecoming practicalities with other spouses, husbands as well as wives nowadays. The children run around in their unnaturally clean best clothes. I managed two glasses before we left, and a strong coffee, and can make intelligent conversation without trying too hard.

The plane lands and the soldiers resemble a caterpillar in uniform as they snake their way across the airstrip. One by one we spot our loved ones, wives, girlfriends, sons.

Everybody cries, even the men. Jack is always the last out of the gate. He has to see all his guys out safely. Eloise runs into his arms and he throws her in the air, twirling her around as she screams with delight, covering his face with kisses.

'My goodness, what a welcome.' He blinks the tears from his eyes. 'I hardly recognised you. Look how you've grown.'

She giggles. 'Maria-at-nursery said you'd say that.'

I am holding back, pulling my new jacket around me, fiddling with the blue, silk scarf he loves. He has bags under his eyes. They've had a relatively easy tour. Nobody died and the mission was successful. He turns to me. We both smile, slightly embarrassed before we kiss. It's always like this, as though we're on a first date. Jack looks at me, taking everything in before we walk off arm in arm, Eloise skipping around our legs, twirling the buggy behind her.

She chatters on and on as we pass the swings and cross the Green. We're unable to get a word in edgeways. Finally, the three of us are home again. Jack shuts the door. Eloise and the twins go off in search of snacks. I daren't speak in case I break down before we have made it into the living room. We sit down. Only now do I notice the sparkling glitter on the hearth rug and the elephant-shaped rubber which Eloise bought for Jack from the waterpark.

'We need to talk,' says Jack. Jack isn't the talking kind. Not about deep, serious things. 'I haven't been managing without you. And I can't get Ben out of my mind. I miss him all the time.'

'You do? Honestly?' Jack organises battles and campaigns. He commands troops. Can he be suffering like me? 'You miss Ben?'

'Of course, I do. Ricky Hooper named his new baby Benjamin. I wanted to hit him.'

Before I can respond Eloise shouts from the kitchen.

'Mummy, this blackcurrant juice tastes funny.'

'NO!' I scream. 'No! Stop! Spit it out. Now! Stupid, stupid, stupid.'

Eloise crumples. She drops the beaker as though she were drinking poison, the wine splashing down the wall. Jack looks askance at me, half critically, half terrified.

'Are you calling *yourself* stupid again, Mummy?' she trembles, catching her breath. 'Or me? I'm *not* stupid and Maria-at-nursery says it's wrong to call people rude names.'

'And Maria-at-nursery is right, my lovely. You're not stupid. But sometimes Mummy is.'

'Verity, what on earth's going on? What is she drinking?'

'Jack. I'm so sorry. We do need to talk. I'm not managing well either. I'm not managing at all. I cry at night and I hide bottles of wine in strange places and I can't cope with the simplest thing and I miss. . .'

The words tumble out in a stream of consciousness.

'I think, I think I may be an alcoholic.'

25. Beer Bottles and Knives

Isobel and Jim were two people for whom the loss of a child changed their lives forever. Isobel's anger at the needless death of her son, Louis, was a continual thread running through her life for years. The saving grace was the birth of her grandchildren.

'Damn you. Go in!' Isobel rams the final invitation card into the stiff, white envelope.

Is that the best word, invitation? Invitations should evoke joy and excitement, parties, weddings, anniversaries. Who wants to be invited to a funeral, especially when the star is shy of thirty? She's only had to address half a dozen to the few dinosaurs who don't have an email address, a Facebook page, or an Instagram account, to those who will want a formal memento, a proper announcement. Louis' godmother, great uncle Stan, Jim's parents. She's not telling them anything new for the tragedy is public news. It made a good story in the red tops. The teenage gang, Louis' heroics, the knives, and the blood. So much blood.

Two funerals in the space of three months is unfair but Mum was eighty-four and ready to go. Louis was in his prime with everything to live for. The raised texture of the envelope, the thick card, takes her back to an earlier time and a different card, one with blue balloons and coloured bunting to herald the arrival of the most wonderful baby the world had ever seen. She remembers pushing a stack into the postbox on the corner, dropping them into neighbours' letter boxes, hoping she'd bump into old friends so she could show off her son. *Jim and Isobel are delighted to announce the arrival of Louis James, born 27th August 1979 at St Luke's Maternity Hospital, 7lb 11 oz.* She'd found one in her Mum's treasure box nestled beside a pile of Louis' letters and drawings. 'Please will you nit me red gluvs?' the top one read. Three decades had passed since that Bank Holiday Monday when he took his first breath. She remembered every minute of the day, the sweltering, airless heat. Pushing and screaming, sweating and swearing, using words she didn't like to admit she knew until he had squelched out in time for tea. Even Jim had cried.

'He's adorable,' the auxiliary nurse had said as she pushed the perspex cradle to the ward. 'Does he have a name yet?'

'Louis. We've called him Louis.'

'What a coincidence. You must have known.'

'Known what?'

It is five days since Isobel glimpsed the uniforms coming down the path. She knew from the sombre faces that this was more than a routine house call.

'There must be a mistake,' said Jim. 'He's on leave, on holiday with Vicky. They're in London. Celebrating his birthday. He can't be dead.'

'Yes,' said Isobel. 'They're dropping in tomorrow on the way home. Something about good news. Here's the postcard.'

They would not be dropping in to share good news. Ever again. It was true. A brawl outside a pub. A group of teenage girls threatened by a mob. Beer bottles and knives. His life was over in an instant.

It is three days since the efficient and well-meaning Joanna from the RAF called, leaving them with brochures and contact numbers, call us any time, night or day, and the promise to return soon. Louis was one of their own. They were proud of him and what he'd done. Isobel wanted to shake her and scream. 'He's not yours. He's mine.' Instead, she kept her cool, thanked her and closed the door behind her. Then she stood still, catching her breath, concentrating on the photo on the mantelpiece. Grainy and badly focussed, but her favourite. Jim was perched awkwardly on the hospital bed, hideous brown and yellow curtains in the background, holding the blue bundle like a bomb primed to explode at the slightest movement. Perhaps if she keeps her eyes on it and pretends nothing has happened, Louis will walk through the door and she will see his understated smile and hear his quiet laugh.

For years, she'd wasted time thinking about the dangers which might await him if she took her eyes off him for a minute. Who would have thought playschool could be traumatic? Not for the three-year-old, running off, waving goodbye without a backward glance, but for her, trudging home, surreptitiously wiping tears from her eyes, only relaxing three hours later when he ran back into her arms, clutching an unidentifiable painting or sticky model. Louis had scraped his knees and bumped his head falling off the slide. Nothing bad had ever happened at nursery, but she always feared the worst.

When his class went to the Isle of Wight for three whole days, she lay awake every night. The coach might crash, the driver might be a pervert with a penchant for blond, nine-year-old boys, a mad axeman might break into the dormitory at midnight, or the ferry capsize. And then there were the teenage girls, drawn to his generous nature and adolescent charm. There was a constant supply of them in the garden, in his bedroom, hanging out, eating pizza, ringing, calling around under some pretext or another. They all wanted his attention, they all wanted a piece of him. Jim said nothing but she knew he was proud when he saw the way the girls admired his son and how Louis took care of them with a casual selflessness beyond his years. For Isobel, it was another step towards losing him to the big, wide world.

From the moment he had told them about the RAF stand at the Rowan House careers' fair and the keen recruiting officer waxing lyrical about exceptional training, making a difference, and travelling the world, she had feared the worst.

'Aircrew. I'm going to be a pilot.'

'How about communications and intelligence,' she said. *Sitting in a safe office analysing information.* 'Right up your street.'

'Or what about becoming a medic? You've always been good at sciences,' said Jim. *In a nice, clean operating theatre rather than a vulnerable aeroplane.* They told themselves he would change his mind or fail a crucial exam, be colourblind or have flat feet, but he applied, won a scholarship, and started officer training.

'A natural leader,' said his Commanding Officer, at the passing out parade. Isobel cried tears of pride at his success and tears of desperation every time he was posted abroad. She and Jim waited anxiously for the news he had landed safely, a message he was still in one piece. When the long-anticipated knock at the door eventually came, they were shell-shocked. He was home. Off duty. In England. They had let their guard down.

A brawl outside a pub. Some teenage girls threatened by a mob. Beer bottles and knives. All over in an instant. Except it isn't. And never will be.

Eighteen months later, Isobel is slumped on the sofa. In the corner, the TV is on and she can see Prince Charles making a speech and a crowd applauding. The stars and stripes are flying. She reaches for the remote. The anniversary of nine/eleven is being celebrated and he is describing how angry he was when his beloved uncle, Louis Mountbatten, was killed and the hatred he had harboured for the terrorists. She is sure about when it happened because Louis was born on the same day, at the same time. She remembers the teenage boat boy who was enjoying his first, and last, summer holiday job.

Prince Charles is saying that revenge is not sweet. That there must be a better way. We should forgive and forget.

'He was your *uncle*,' she screams at the screen. 'Not your only son.'

She will never be able to speak about finding strength or moving on, or drawing a line, or any other trite phrases that pepper his speech. She doesn't want his patronising wisdom. She wants her son back.

CCTV captured everything. The boys who killed Louis were found and tried. Too young to serve a proper sentence, though. Titus Belvoir Q.C. explained the judge's hands were tied. She still wants revenge. She will never forgive them. Ever.

Five years have passed since Isobel's world was destroyed by the flash of a blade and a broken bottle. His murderers have been released. They will be out there living their lives, going out with girls, having babies, and planning their futures. Five years have passed since Vicky, barely able to speak in the depths of grief, told them the news Louis promised on his last postcard. They were expecting a baby. *She* was expecting a baby, she corrected herself. There was no Louis to hold her hand or share the fear or the excitement. No Louis to get up for the midnight feed or tell her she was doing a good job.

A beautiful, healthy girl arrived. Isla Isobel. The tears streamed down Jim's face as he gazed into his granddaughter's blurry eyes. She was perfect but Louis would never know. It was too much to bear. He would have been such a good dad. Vicky was a loving mother and made superhuman efforts to stop the tragedy defining her life, but as Isobel watched her doing everything on her own, she decided she would never forgive those boys if she lived to be a hundred. Grieving was exhausting. Bitterness was debilitating but she would not give it up.

Then gradually, Isobel felt herself changing. Perhaps Prince Charles had a point. Time wasn't *a great healer* and she would never *get over it* but revenge was pointless and destructive. She had steeled herself to welcome Ted when he came with Vicky and Isla for Sunday lunch. She had forced a fixed smile on her face, and watched Isla leading him around the garden like a pet pony, Ted on all fours obeying her every command. She knew it was only a matter of time before he became Isla's new dad because Vicky had started wearing lipstick again.

Tonight, she and Jim were babysitting. She smiled down at four-year-old Isla ('four and a *half*, Grandma') and stroked her blonde curls. They had finished *Peter Pan* and turned to her *First Day at School* picture book.

'Guess what, Grandma. Mummy says I can go to proper school after the holidays. I'm too old for Cygnets now. Do you want to see my red sweatshirt with the picture of a swan on the front? I'm going to be in green class and all my friends are coming with me.'

'Goodness me, Isla, slow down a bit. I can't keep up.'

Jim lowered his newspaper and peeked over the top. The school was safe now. Mr Goodman was long since gone. Nothing to be anxious about.

'And Mummy says if I work hard and listen to the teacher I can be anything I want to be when I'm older. Maybe a doctor or a vet or a hairdresser or a pilot like Daddy was.'

Isobel looks at her precious granddaughter and wonders, as she does every day, at her likeness to Louis. The same smile, the same blond curls, his final gift to the world, the child who would bring life to a world he would never share. A brawl outside a pub. Teenage girls threatened by a mob. Beer bottles and knives. All over in an instant. Except it isn't. And never will be.

26. Jesus and Father Christmas

Every child is precious. George was extra-special because he
was the miracle baby Rachel and Steve never expected to have
but their 'little professor' threw up particular challenges.
Children on the autistic spectrum (and even as I write that
somebody will be telling me the language is wrong) need to
be understood. Watch Chris Packham as he walks around a
primary school pointing out the traps for people like him and
you'll see what I mean.

The new headteacher at Swan Meadows Primary asked
to meet George's parents in early December. She wasn't
exactly new. She'd been the deputy for a while before being
promoted. Steve was away on the oil rig as usual, which left
Rachel to face the ordeal alone. Her sister, Daisy offered to
go with her. She was, she said, George's godmother and
his aunt, but Rachel, fearful of unfair comparisons with his
perfect cousins, said she must cope by herself.

'Thanks for coming,' said Mrs Marshall.

'Is anything wrong?' Rachel ran her fingers through her
untamed, curly hair.

'Nothing we can't deal with,' the Head said, smile fixed
in place, auburn hair shiny and well-behaved, nails pink
and glossy.

'Miss Lewis, our SENCO, is the expert but I wanted
to sit in, too. I need to be sure we're doing our best for
George.'

Rachel frowned and was even more worried. The
previous head had never had time to be this interested.

'George was assessed before he started in reception as gifted and talented,' said Mrs Marshall. 'He's very advanced in numeracy and literacy and talented in music. Not many five-year-olds have passed a violin exam.'

'He's only been in year 1 for a term but there's never been a problem before, not when he was in nursery or reception,' said Rachel

Miss Lewis nodded.

'So?' said Rachel, mirroring the posed smile.

'I'm concerned about his relationships with the other children,' said Mrs Marshall. 'And what he's telling them about Christmas.'

Rachel could hazard a guess as to what was coming next.

'George is a born leader. He organised extra rehearsals for the nativity play in the playground and because he'd memorised all the words, he was able to help everybody.'

'It made playtime manageable for him because he was in control and, surprisingly, the children loved it,' said Miss Lewis.

'But?' asked Rachel. Mrs Marshall took a breath, as though she was thinking about how to phrase the sentence.

'Two or three of the younger children are upset because George has told them the baby Jesus is a *figment of their imagination* – those were his very words – and if Mary had given birth in a stable, she would have died from a post-natal infection.'

'He says the wise men, if they existed, would have come on elephants, not camels,' said Miss Lewis 'and angels aren't real because nobody has ever seen one since. George says they are as unlikely to exist as Santa Claus.'

'Rev Bethan is rarely lost for words, but even she struggled to come up with a convincing response,' said the Head.

She paused to let her words sink in, but Rachel wasn't surprised. This was one incident among many experienced by a mother with a child on the autistic spectrum. She had waited so long for a baby. Several failed attempts at IVF, endless injections, and clinic appointments had led to nothing until, one miraculous morning, the little blue line told her she was expecting. With George, the mini professor who now shared their home, she'd got more than she'd bargained for. She had never told anybody she wished he were a bit more *normal* but, occasionally, she did.

'Now George may well be right,' Mrs Marshall. 'And he says Uncle Titus is a lawyer and agrees with him so it must be true. Theologians would find him an informed sparring partner, and debating is a laudable occupation . . .'

'. . . but not with children in Reception,' said Rachel. She wished he was like other children, singing songs about poo and bums and willies, counting to ten, and getting the numbers in the wrong order. She longed for conversations about Bluey and Paw Patrol. Not Beethoven.

'What do you advise, then? He can't help being different. He takes everything in and thinks about it until he's made his mind up. To him, the idea of angels and the notion of Father Christmas are irrational.'

Mrs Marshall nodded. 'George is a kind boy. He is very empathetic, but he can't stop himself from telling the truth.'

Rachel had heard all this before, from the GP, from specialists, and from well-meaning relatives who had no first-hand experience of living with an autistic child. Daisy had strong views and theories but Titus understood

George better than her and listened to him. He treated him as a miniature colleague, like an adult partner in chambers. Privately, she suspected he was envious. If anybody was going to have a genius child, it should have been him.

She loved her little gift of a child and she loved their second miracle, Lily but it wasn't easy holding the family together when one child was playing with a doll's house and the other memorising the length of all the rivers in Africa before breakfast.

'I want him to fit in,' she said. 'We both worry he won't have any friends and will end up isolated. What's to be done then?'

'We can't ask him to live a lie and you don't want him to stop asking questions, even if you can't answer them,' said Miss Lewis. 'What do you think he asked me when the band played the national anthem on Remembrance Day?'

'I can guess because he asked me, too. *Why did God save the Queen?*'

'And yesterday, he asked why you never see a sheep wearing glasses, and whether they have twenty-twenty vision.'

Rachel found herself laughing. 'And don't tell me, he went on to give a lecture about how sheep have fifty-four chromosomes and goats have sixty.'

'Yes, and how ravens take out lambs' eyes,' said Miss Lewis. 'I had to ask him to write everything down to give the children a break and me time to draw breath.'

Rachel sighed. She was relieved that the staff liked him, despite his peculiar ways.

'Now, I know we did discuss whether George should miss out year one and go straight into year two but I don't recommend it,' said Mrs Marshall.

'I'm not keen either,' said Rachel. 'He reads like an eight-year-old but emotionally and physically he's like every other six-year-old.'

'Well, perhaps we should review things. Miss Lewis and I have been reconsidering the options.'

Rachel shifted in the seat and folded her arms across her chest.

'Don't even think about suggesting homeschooling. Over my dead body.' There *would* be a dead body if they went down that route. 'I don't have the patience or the capacity. He's just turned six and he knows more about some things than I do.'

'Nothing was further from my mind,' said Mrs Marshall. 'Not many teachers favour that. But we can consider other things.'

Rachel sat back. Here was a person with authority who was interested in George but as a person and not an anomaly. She even had plans to make life easier.

'We could investigate other mainstream schools with LCRs – Language and Communication Resources. Or consider a mix-and-match. Mornings with a tutor, afternoons in school. But we need to do something if only to give Miss Lewis a break.'

'Would you do that?'

Mrs Marshall smiled. 'As long as nobody asks me about the budget. Manor House Primary has a special unit for gifted and talented children. I think you visited, didn't you?'

Rachel had done. The approach was narrow and focused and the children were all the same.

'I was keen to keep him in an ordinary school,' she said.

'Miss Lewis says children can go in the morning and then to mainstream school after lunch. It's not all or nothing.'

'You're not saying you want George to leave?'

'Absolutely not,' said Mrs Marshall. 'Who would play the violin for the carol service?'

Rachel knew George and Lily would be surprised to find she had driven to school to meet them.

'Why aren't we walking home as usual?' asked Lily.

'Because we all deserve a treat. And because I love you. How about pizza and chocolate ice cream for tea?'

'Cool,' said George, quietly registering that today was Tuesday and wondering what was wrong. 'But Mummy, every sixty-three grams of Margherita pizza has 173 calories. More, if you have pepperoni and pineapple. I read the box last time we had one at home.'

'Just this once won't hurt. You'll run it off in the garden.'

Lily was unmoved by her brother's culinary knowledge and had no interest in counting calories.

'Me and George haven't had pizza for ages.'

'George and *I*,' said George.

27. The Cats

When I first started taking funerals, I was surprised by the complexity of emotions surrounding loss. I hadn't realized that dead or alive, a person's legacy would last forever. Carole's story led me into uncharted land but Roger and Verity, who knew all about grief, helped Carole start again.

When Bethan arrived at the hall to help Roger prepare for the bereavement group meeting, Carole was already there waiting outside hopping nervously from one foot to the other. Her eyes darted around as though she were expecting danger.

'Mum died like when I was eleven remember' she said as they danced around one another in the entrance hall. 'Double-whammy. Losing Dad as well. I don't think I can go in there again.'

Bethan said she would ask Verity to sit beside Carole if she was worried about meeting other people, and then, maybe, she, Bethan, could visit Carole at home. She'd had her losses, too, she said. Smiled her most appealing smile. Took in the picture of the thin, dishevelled woman with lanky hair, a ripped tee shirt (*not* a fashion statement), and skinny black jeans. Saw how fragile she was.

'Do you mind cats?' Clearly, that was a deal-breaker.

'Love them. Mine's called KitKat.'

'Like the chocolate bar?'

'Exactly. She turned up out of the blue, and marched up the path as though she owned the place just as I was eating one.'

'OK, then. You can come.'

A few days later, Bethan drove to the outer edge of Lower Swannery and stood on the doorstep of the ground-floor maisonette where, until recently, Carole had lived with her dad. The net curtains were grubby. The green door was scuffed, and the number 5 hung at an angle. Carole opened the door a few inches and peered out, wary and suspicious.

'Hi, Carole. It's me. Bethan. Is it still convenient?' Carole opened the door a fraction more and let her in.

'Goodness me, what a lot of cats.' Down the dark hallway, she could see four or five dishevelled animals of various colours and sizes. They were rubbing themselves on the bannisters, scratching the skirting board, and, oh my life, a ginger one was defecating in the space under the stairs. Could smells cause you to pass out? Bethan grabbed a handful of tissues from her bag and pretended to blow her nose.

'Must have a bit of a cold coming,' she said.

No wonder Carole had been reluctant for her to visit. Bethan squashed her anger. Why did some people have to live in such awful conditions? And what had Carole's dad been doing to let things get to this state? Fathers were meant to protect their daughters and care for them; but that was God's job, too and where was he when you needed him?

Carole led the way into the front room which bore all the signs of having been the victim of a violent, presumably feline, demolition campaign. Carole sat in a frayed armchair and Bethan perched on an upright, wooden chair. She wondered if she would ever be able to wear her trousers again. She offered a silent prayer of thanks that Carole didn't offer her a drink. Cats sidled in and out of the door, emerged from behind the sideboard, leapt onto Carole's lap, and off again.

'How many cats do you have exactly?' she asked, over an ear-splitting cacophony, not sure she wanted to know the answer.

'Twenty-nine,' said Carole as if that were normal. 'We don't have them done. They like breeding, and they're good at it. There's more in the dining room.'

She leapt up with surprising energy and beckoned Bethan to follow her past the piles of poo, fresh and old, towards the back of the house where a door was hanging off its hinges. She lifted it by the handle and scraped it across the floor making enough of a gap to get through. The dining table, one of those old, square, extendable jobs with solid legs, was covered with damp and discoloured newspaper. A couple of enamel pie dishes were half filled with water of a dubious colour. When Bethan saw a minute insect jumping from one stringy black cat to another, she backed out quickly.

She struggled to count the creatures as they were wandering in and out, entwining themselves around the curtains and each other, but twenty-nine didn't sound like an exaggeration. And anyway, what's another cat or two between friends? She dreaded to think what might be going on in the kitchen, or how many others were prowling around the neighbourhood seeking whom they may devour. They returned to the living room, Carole embracing two jet-black cats, one in each arm. As Bethan trod carefully behind, she registered two more doors leading off the hallway.

'You don't let the cats in the bedrooms?'

'Oh yeah. They've always had the smaller one to themselves.'

Perhaps Carole used to sleep on the sofa. Intuition told her that wasn't true, but she had no idea what to say next. She must have missed the module on incest at theological college.

'Forget about the cats for a minute. Tell me about your dad again.'

Carole talked about her dad's job in the Post Office, how he liked a pint and was an avid Spurs supporter. How he never coped with losing his wife when Carole was eleven and he was thirty-eight, still a young man.

'I told you all this before the funeral,' she said.

'I know, but I keep so much information in my head. It helps to hear your story over and over. I'm wondering if we could meet again. In Meadow Park. Out in the fresh air. We can have an ice cream or a coffee. My treat.' She would gladly pay for every choc ice or coke to escape the cats.

'Good idea. Dad went there all the time. He loved watching the kiddies on the swings.'

They continued to meet in the park until the weather drove them into the warmth of Luigi and Carlo's café. Carole had agreed to have the cats neutered and to re-home a few, but she was not, she said, a *vulnerable adult* whatever the social worker thought. Her dad was not, like, a criminal, so why on earth had the police been involved? Especially since he was dead. She and Dad loved each other and she hadn't minded missing school. She was, like, rubbish at most things anyway.

'But haven't you ever wanted a job? To meet friends your own age? You can't spend the rest of your life caring for cats.' Bethan was tempted to say Carole would be attractive if she tidied herself up, and spent a bit on shampoo, but stopped herself just in time. You weren't allowed to say things like that.

'How can I get a job? I can't do anything.'

'Maybe you can do more than you think.'

'Like what?'

'Look after cats; or other animals. Or even people.'

There was a small smile, a germ of interest.

'Like how?'

'You could start by volunteering at the cats' rescue centre or their shop in Church Street. Or advertise to sit for pets when people are away. Or become a carer.'

Carole bit a nail. Pushed the half-empty mug of tea away. Opened her mouth to speak, but thought better of it.

'I don't think so. You see I can't. They wouldn't take me, would they?'

'You'd have to train; learn the ropes.'

'But I'm such a wreck,' she said. 'They wouldn't want people like me.'

Bethan breathed another silent prayer of thanksgiving.

'Well, you're not a wreck. You need help to smarten up a bit. Have you ever seen those makeover shows on telly?'

'Like, where they take a fat, frumpy person and turn them into something half decent. Like Cinderella and the fairy godmother.'

'I wouldn't put it quite like that, but, that sort of thing, yes.'

'No money,' said Carole. 'I get benefits and Dad had a bit put by, but those things cost the earth.'

'I'm not thinking about bringing Gok Wan in.'

'Gok what?'

'Never mind. We can easily find you smarter jeans and tops.'

'Yeah?' The nails were stuffed in the mouth again.

'And Locks is always advertising for models for their trainees. Dead cheap. What do you say?'

Carole allowed herself a smile, blushed. She was pretty, Bethan thought. She would ask Verity to take her under her wing a bit. Be sure to chat with her at the next bereavement group meeting. Do them both a power of good.

28. *Johanna Grace*

*Women like Magda, Audrey and Fiona can be found in any
parish and can be edgy and awkward but they are kind and
caring at heart once you get below the surface. Verity and
Jack needed all the help they could get and their story had a
happy ending.*

'Magda, is it right, what was in the parish mag? Do you
really want all my old bras?'

Verity and Eloise were following two women into
church. Verity stopped in her tracks. Had she misheard?

'Yes, please, Fiona. Any will do. There's a breast cancer
charity that can get £700 a tonne for them.'

Verity laughed out loud. The women, both well into
their seventies, turned around, paused. They hesitated,
unsure how to respond. When Magda smiled, Fiona
followed suit.

'What's funny, Mummy?' said Eloise.

'There's Sophie and her dad. Do you want to go into
Little Fishes with them?'

'Yes. But I wish my Daddy would come home and take
me.'

'He'll be home soon, sweetie. Promise.'

Six weeks was a long time for a four-year-old to wait.
A long time for an adult to wait. She had a hunch that he
might appear sooner than planned if his last messages had
been anything to go by. Something was wrong but she
couldn't put her finger on it. His work was difficult and

sometimes dangerous so he was probably concerned about the latest tour. His texts were even briefer than usual and he never usually forgot to say 'love you' or 'miss you' even when things were going badly. Yesterday, they'd managed to speak for a few minutes and she was sure he'd been crying. He was crossing off the days until he'd be home, he said. By then, she calculated she'd be past the twelve-week watershed.

It was too soon to be counting sleeps. Too many lonely nights to go. Too many days to fill. Not too soon to be thinking about names, though. The best bit about being pregnant. Her reverie was interrupted when one of the women touched her arm.

'Come and sit with us. I'm Magda and this is Fiona. Have you been before?'

Verity smiled, thanked them, apologised for laughing about the bras.

'It's not the kind of conversation you expect to hear walking into church,' she said, as she sat down beside them. 'We have been before, but not very often. Sophie's persuaded Eloise she's missing out. And the chapel on the base is like a barn, and the services a bit. . .'

'Formal?' suggested Magda. 'Stuffy?' said Fiona, speaking over one another.

Verity smiled. She felt refreshed by the different atmosphere of the civilian world where there were fewer uniforms and rules and where she wasn't expected to conform. She sat still and let the queasiness pass. Set her mind on higher things. Verity was unsure what she believed and hoped nobody would ask her. She did know she was an inadequate kind of Christian. Never read her bible and only ever prayed in desperation. She was nothing like the glowing sunbeam Jesus wanted her to be but it was hard to glow all the time. Easy to be joyful when everything was going well. Easy then to appreciate the imagery – the living water, the bread of life, the fruit of the vine. But when you were drowning and there was no bread and the fruit of the vine had taken over every waking moment, what about those times? Where was God then? Where was God when your baby was dying?

She followed Magda's lead, stood when she did, sat when she did, and let the words and music swell over her head, grateful for the time away from Eloise's sweet but constant chatter. She drifted down the aisle with everybody else to receive communion. As she was returning to her seat the choir began to sing 'For the beauty of the earth'. She'd never heard that version before. There was no early warning, no time to dissemble. The tears ran down her cheeks. She knelt on the tapestry cushion, covered her face with her hands, and pretended she was deep in prayer. Thank goodness Magda had gone to make the coffee. She would have dashed for home but the little fishes were straggling in from the hall clasping their creations, ready to wow their parents with their offerings. Eloise would never forgive her if she weren't there.

'Look, Mummy. This is a dove. He's called Harry. Did you know there were doves in the bible? Can we get a dove?'

Fiona made encouraging noises and told Eloise what a clever girl she was. Sophie rushed up and grabbed her hand, offering biscuits and squash. 'You can have orange or blackcurrant.'

Verity, unable to speak, nodded at Eloise. Orange or blackcurrant. 'I'll catch you up,' she said. She needed a minute to compose herself before joining the coffee queue. She breathed in, out, in, out. Her phone vibrated in her pocket. She pulled it out. Jack? They'd only spoken yesterday. A text. 'Coming home. Nothing to worry about. xx'

Nothing to worry about? What did that mean? He wouldn't have done anything wrong. He gave no date or time. She stared at the screen, reading and re-reading the brief message, searching for the subtext.

'You're Verity, aren't you?' said a voice. 'I've seen you at school. Didn't you bring your little girl to see the poppies? And Ben was your little boy, wasn't he?'

'You know about Ben?'

'Vicars get to know about everything,' said Bethan.

'I thought only Maria-at-nursery and Miss Webber in Reception knew everything.'

Bethan laughed. 'Everything OK? You look a bit shocked.'

Verity shrugged her shoulders. Forced herself to smile. 'Not quite with it this morning. Everything's fine.'

'Yes, of course, it is. But can I pop in tomorrow anyway?'

Conversation was a bit stilted to start with. Bethan had never been married and had no children. How could she understand? But Verity was surprised to find herself telling this unusual vicar about Ben, the drinking, the hidden bottles and how difficult it was to resist a daily fix. Bethan didn't throw her hands in the air. She sympathised with her fears about Jack's state of mind. Fears that were magnified, she suggested, by the distance between them. Said it wasn't unusual for people to find all kinds of unhelpful strategies to cope with the crap they experienced.

'Anyway,' said Verity, when she was tired of talking about Merlot and thinking about Jack, 'I enjoyed church yesterday in a funny kind of way. Thanks for coming round.'

'Magda and Fiona, they're a bit forceful, but they don't miss a trick and they're all heart once you get through the shell. They had the idea you might like to come to our bereavement group. Roger, one of our churchwardens is the facilitator. You couldn't find a less threatening person.'

'Bereavement group? But Ben died ages ago. Won't people think I should be over it by now?' *And everybody will be old,* she thought.

'You'll never *get over it,* will you? Roger understands that more than most. He lost a daughter. The people who come are a mixed bag but they have one thing in common so it works pretty well.'

Despite her reservations, Verity turned up at the hall for the next session. Bethan was right. Roger had a real knack with people. Gave off an air of quiet confidence which put others at ease. He wouldn't be thrown by anything anybody said, however awful. They *were* a mixed bag for sure: mostly over sixty but one in her fifties and a woman called Carole who looked about thirty. Carole had lost her father, Bernard his wife, Louise her son *and* her husband. Hearing their stories was comforting, knowing she wasn't alone. Talking about Ben gave him value and identity. By the end of the meeting, she was exhausted but glad she'd come.

'Jack's coming home earlier than expected,' she told her new friends as they cleared away the chairs. 'I'm going to tell Eloise after school. She'll be over the moon.' She didn't add that *she* was terrified. Kept that under wraps.

No, he wasn't injured. He'd been given compassionate leave. Verity was still confused. The night before he'd left, he'd seemed like his old self. The image of Ben which had always come between them was fainter. They'd made love as they had in the past, with ease and with no inhibitions. In her mind, the night of passion marked a milestone. Since then, what communication they'd had was awkward, interspersed with uncomfortable silences.

Eloise couldn't have been more excited if Father Christmas himself had collected her on his sleigh with a reindeer or two. She danced around the playground clapping and shouting the news to her friends.

'Daddy can take me to church, can't he, like Sophie's Daddy. Let's go home and make a cake straightaway, Mummy, in case he comes tonight. I'm so excited I could. . .' she held her breath, trying to finish the sentence, but did a handstand instead, fell ungraciously onto the ground and giggled uncontrollably.

A few days later, in the middle of the morning, Verity saw him through the kitchen window getting out of a Land Rover. She rushed to the front door, flung it wide open, put her arms around him and led him indoors. His cheeks were sunken, he was unshaven. He'd lost weight. She struggled to understand what he was trying to say and, finally, took him by the hand, moved towards the sofa and pushed him gently down into the cushions.

'It's all right,' she said. 'Everything's all right. Sit here while I make us a strong coffee. Don't move!' She spoke with mock severity, but with a gentleness she usually reserved for Eloise. Verity listened as Jack recounted the conversation with his C.O. '*No shame in expressing your emotions,*' Jack mimicked. '*No shame in grieving. Deal with it now or it will come back and bite your arse. You're no good to me like this.*' He blew his nose. 'I've never failed at anything before but he was right. I was becoming a liability.'

'Well, you're not a liability to me, and Eloise will be ecstatic when we collect her from school. Whatever we need to do, we'll do. Whatever help you need, we'll find. I'm just glad to have you here, to have the chance to face the demons together.'

Jack stared into the middle distance, his hands grasping the mug. His mouth opened as though he were struggling for the right words but changed his mind at the last minute.

'Don't say anything, my love. Just listen. There's a particular reason we need to work this out. I can't have you being under par when the baby comes.'

Johanna Grace was born in the birthing pool on her due date in the hospital where Eloise and Ben had been born. Verity held her close and stroked her head, gazed into her tiny, brown eyes. Jack couldn't stop crying, his shoulders heaving, his eyes red. She was perfect. Verity was perfect. If Ben was in heaven looking down, he hoped he'd as be proud of his new sister as he knew Eloise would be. Proud and self-important, bossy and chatty.

On the third day, Carole from the bereavement group turned up on the doorstep. Her hair was short and spiky.

'It's called Edgy Pixie,' she said. 'D'you like it?'

'You look amazing.'

'Thanks. Been shopping. And while I was there, I bought this for the baby at the charity shop but it's new.'

Verity pulled the tiny, white babygrow out of the crumpled paper bag. The label was still attached and round and round the centre marched a circle of silver penguins.

29. The Bauhaus Cradle

Our experiences (and those of our ancestors) live on in our hearts and minds for a long time and shape our approach to people and circumstances. Slowly, I absorbed that fact as I learned about my history and reframed my attitudes. Magda's story was both tragic and illuminating. Her enlightened grandchild helped her to let go of her anger and resentment.

You've probably guessed, Bethan. I haven't always been a Christian, but I've always had a strong faith. My Jewish past saw to that. You must have wondered about me. Not many Christians recite the psalms as often as I do and I look Jewish, don't I? Converting to another faith is complicated to say the least. To be honest, it would have been easier if I'd been an atheist, starting from nothing.

My mother, Miriam, was one of the first children to come out of Germany on the Kindertransport. She was fifteen, and her brother was thirteen. He died from tuberculosis quite quickly, but she survived, though she never saw any of her family again. We heard terrible stories about what some of those children went through, but my mother was fortunate. Blessed, I should say. She became the daughter her foster parents never had so they sent her to good schools, fed her well, and encouraged her to take every opportunity they gave her. Eventually, she became a teacher, She married my father, another emigrant, and had me.

Every day, I am thankful for my parents and for the British people who opened their hearts to us but, try as

I might, I've never shaken off the hatred I had for the Germans: not just the soldiers who did those terrible things but all of them, even if they weren't alive at the time. Stupid, wrong, sinful, call it what you will, it goes deep. If you weren't there, and didn't experience that overwhelming fear or the bottomless pit of sorrow at being wrenched away from your family, well, you can't judge.

I remember hearing Father Dominic preaching a sermon on forgiveness once. He was a good preacher and he gave a memorable sermon but what did he know about it? Easy to tell others to forgive when nothing terrible has happened to you. But his words always stuck with me: 'The past is always there, waiting to leap out at you.'

Well, I only talked about my past to Ron. We met in Oxford when he was at university, and I was a new teacher. I wasn't keen on his friends. They were a bit brash and full of themselves but I tagged along because I was dead keen on Ron. Their mission was to convert Jews to Christianity. I laughed out loud when Ron told me. Impossible, I said, and if you've strung me along because of that you can think again. Anyway, he hadn't. He loved me for me. Still does. So here I am, a churchwarden of an Anglican church in an English village. I bet God's laughing his head off.

I've tried hard to forgive my enemies but it's not easy. We also have several prayers for forgiveness, and, in my head, I thought I was making some progress but my heart never caught up. When Father Dominic did what he did, I realized that we all need to live while we can and make amends while there's time. I've finally got there, thanks to Karen, my precious granddaughter.'

Bethan wriggled about a bit, changing position. It was going to be a long story.

'It was a few years ago now. Karen had sent me a birthday card with two tickets for an exhibition. *Germany: Memories of a Nation.* She'd written a note inside saying she and a friend would meet us for tea afterwards. I was livid. Why on earth would we want to go and celebrate Germany? After everything they had done to me and mine. Didn't they teach them anything at school? Ron and I had a bit of an argument. He said good always came from evil, and we would never have met if things had been different, and anyway, Karen had bought the tickets. Wouldn't want to upset her by not going, would we? Then he went for the jugular. Reminded me of how I'd raved about Father Dominic's sermon on forgiveness. It was true. I had. I didn't have a leg to stand on. I gave myself a talking-to and promised Ron I'd go with an open mind. I didn't want to upset Karen. She wasn't to blame.'

Bethan nodded.

'I have to tell you, I was wrong. The exhibition was captivating from the moment I saw the bright yellow VW at the entrance. It was a clever idea to use objects to bring history to life. Far more powerful than words. Ron loved the coin display. I adored the Meissen porcelain. Too gold and decorative for our table but very beautiful. Around every corner, there was a new treasure. Then we saw a hand-copied Bible, the kind the wealthy could afford to buy, long before the birth of the printing press. We take so much for granted. We think nothing of buying books and throwing newspapers away, and we leave religious books lying around as though they were worthless.

But there were two things I shall never forget. The first was the Buchenwald doorway. Makes me sick to think about it. I can hardly find the words.'

But you will, thought Bethan.

'The Germans had painted in red on the inside of the gate *Jedem das Seine*, to each his own. The prisoners were forced to see it every day. My friends or relatives could have been among them. It was the cruellest thing suggesting they were getting what they deserved and shouldn't be making such a fuss. Nobody deserves torture, hunger, and extermination.

Thankfully, as I was on the point of leaving because it was so awful, we went into the next room and almost walked into a beautiful Bauhaus cradle. I keep a postcard on the mantelpiece. Bright and colourful, such a contrast to the dreaded doorway. Ron didn't agree. It was too angular, shiny and metallic for him but to me, the bright blue circle, red square and yellow triangle were vibrant and living. The odd thing was, it was made in 1922. Nearly twenty years before the war. The guards in the prison camp could have slept in a cradle like that. The richer ones, anyway.

I stood there imagining all those German mothers rocking their babies to sleep. Pictured them waving their sons off to war, not knowing if they'd ever see them again. That was the turning point. I realized I'd been wrong to write off a whole nation. The Nazis were evil but they didn't speak for every German person.

We couldn't take anymore, either of us, and we were due to meet Karen. She was waiting for us at the café entrance. Her cheeks were flushed, she was young and healthy, with everything to live for. We ordered black forest gateau and Earl Grey tea. Very cosmopolitan, said Ron. A bit of Germany and a bit of England. We were tucking in when a man skipped the queue and approached our table. He sat down beside Karen without any word of explanation. He had swept-back blond hair and blue metal-framed glasses.

Karen smiled at him and I could see immediately he was smitten. Then, she came out with it, bold as brass. *Grandma, Grandpa, this is Max, my fiancé.*

When he spoke, it was clear he wasn't British.

I come from Dresden, Mrs Robinson, he said. *My parents are there and my two sisters also.* Apparently, he'd proposed a couple of weeks before, going down on one knee in front of the Bauhaus cradle. Karen said everybody clapped and cheered when they realized what was going on. The exhibition united the two nations, he'd said. A sign of hope and unity. Such a grown-up idea, and so moving. He'd given Karen a delicate, silver ring with tiny engraved patterns. His grandmother owned it and it's steeped in family history. I didn't even try to hide the tears. Wept like a child in full view of everybody in the café.

Ron was proud of me, and I hope Father Dominic would have been, too. Whatever he may or may not have done, I valued his opinion. I couldn't stop hugging them both, welcoming him to the family and wittering on about how good the exhibition was. I wasn't even pretending. Max is such a charmer, and they're very well-suited. They haven't let on, but I'm pretty sure Karen is expecting. She has that look about her.

That's my story, then. My life had a tragic and devastating start, but finally, the bitterness was healed and our story had a happy ending.'

30. The Christmas Cards

We've met Isobel before. Here she is moving in and out of reality, still seeking her beloved Louis.

'I'm going to write my Christmas cards this morning,' she says as she lumbers down the stairs, moving sideways like a giant crab, one hand gripping the bannisters, her bag slung across her chest, its contents dangerously close to reaching the bottom before she does.

'We did those yesterday, didn't we? D'you remember? You wrote them all, I addressed the envelopes, you put the stamps on and they're all ready to go. Six weeks ahead of time.'

'Did we? All of them?'

'You've done Becca, the hairdresser, the woman from church who brings the magazine, Eliza down the road and Pru's Bernard. Who else is there?'

'Oh. We've written them all, have we?'

'And addressed the envelopes and put the stamps on and there they are on the dresser waiting to be posted.'

'Did we do one for Louis? He'll be home for Christmas, won't he.'

A statement, not a question. It brooks no challenge.

'Where did you say your nearest post box is? Shall we post them today?'

'Not yet. It's only the eighteenth of November. But there's the post box, Isobel,' I say, pointing across the road through the dining room window. 'Can you see?'

Well, you could if you had the right glasses on, I don't say. She has five pairs in the overflowing bag which she empties and repacks three or four times a day. Nobody is sure what they are for or whether they achieve anything. Perhaps we should send the ones you don't use to Africa, I suggest, but she won't relinquish a single pair. You never know when you might need them. She has the beige ones in the tapestry case and the mottled beige ones in the velvet drawstring bag while the light beige ones are temporarily homeless. She has another pair on and a fifth nestles in a bright red case.

'Remember, red for reading,' I have said more times than I can count.

'Can't read now,' she says. 'The print's too small. Shall we do the Christmas cards after breakfast?'

We are a few days into her visit. I don't know the Latin word for murdering your mother-in-law but I am sure the tabloid press will find or invent one if the police discover her slumped over a bowl of strange-smelling parsnip soup or smothered by the 16.5 tog winter duvet.

'It's easier for a woman to do things for her,' says Ted. 'I can't help her in the shower or tidy her knickers away.' No, I think. How convenient. She's not even my mother. My mum never lost her mind, not until the last few days. Her body gave up on her long before she was ready to die but she had all her faculties.

'It's all the fish I ate as a child,' she used to say. 'Good for the brains and easy to get during the war.'

I don't know why I've brought that up again, because I've threatened to move out if Isobel says 'during the war' one more time. Every day, whatever the latest news, whatever the topic, whoever has died, the one certainty is that 'during the war' life was better, worse, tougher or more dangerous. I wouldn't mind but she's not old enough to remember much about the war. She's regurgitating what *her* mother said when she was old, retrieving long-lost memories that aren't even her own.

Nobody had time for mental health issues and anxiety then. Not like the kids queueing up for counselling nowadays, vying for attention. Women didn't complain about loneliness and depression when their men were far away risking life and limb. They kept the home fires burning and carried on. Children didn't have proper schooling for six years and you didn't hear them complaining about unequal opportunities or questioning their exam grades. And as for saying you wanted to be a boy when you were very clearly a girl, well, there were no words.

It's ironic. It was my idea to go and collect her earlier than we'd planned. I who reminded him to bring extra clothes for her. She may need to stay for longer if the weather turns. Don't forget the blue badge and walker. Fresh air is good for her. It was me who organised a month's worth of blood pressure tablets just in case.

To be fair, she's been a perfect grandmother to Isla and Oscar and a perfect mother-in-law. When Louis died – was killed – she stepped in and rescued me even though she was heartbroken herself. She never resented Ted when I married him three years after Isla was born and she's treated Oscar like he was her own flesh and blood. Never interfering, always ready to drop everything and come down to help when the children were little and we were exhausted, as we were all the time. Like my mum, she was a rock. Always ready with a mop or a broom, brandishing the iron like there was no tomorrow, sweeping the leaves or clearing out the playroom. I've no complaints; but neither has she, I hope.

Thank goodness, she's forgotten about the Christmas cards. She wanders around the house with a damp cloth and an aerosol can. She reminds me of the roaring lion in the bible seeking whom he may devour. More than once, in the nick of time, I've stopped her from spraying it on her hair. The smell of lavender wax permeates everywhere as she has polished the dining table three times in as many days. The parquet flooring has never been as shiny and Juno, the labradoodle, is slumped in her bed, holding her paws up in surrender. If she could, she'd be waving a white flag.

'Juno's been out three times this morning,' I say, stroking her head – the dog's, not Isobel's. 'She's exhausted.'

'Well, who took her out?' she asks, folding her arms and doing that thing she does with her lips when she is put out. 'That's my job. I always take her for a walk when I'm here.' She sounds like Isla and Oscar arguing over who's eaten the last doughnut or taken the wrong school rucksack.

The days are shorter now. By about half past three, we persuade her to sit down with a cup of tea and a ginger nut to watch TV. She doesn't want to sleep, she says, but more often than not, she rests her eyes after the exhaustion of the morning. Dinner and more TV take care of the remainder of the day, and then we begin the slow ascent of the stairs and another bedtime ritual. It's like being on a treadmill at the gym unable to reach the off button. Luckily for all of us, she sleeps like a log and our nights are our own until, at about eight, she begins to sing. Well, she sounds more like the muezzin calling people to prayer, but less tuneful.

'I don't want to be old,' I say to Ted when we are snuggled under the duvet.

'Well, that's kind of difficult, Vicky' he says, turning another page of his thriller. 'Think of what you'd miss. I'm not taking you to Switzerland and I can't stand the sight of blood. Any other bright ideas?'

I pull the quilt up, turn out my bedside light, and breathe deeply. 'Sad, isn't it? She's gone downhill quickly.'

'It'll be us before long,' said Ted. 'Our kids will be having these same conversations with their spouses, finding jobs for us to do where we can't do any harm or break anything. Passing us on from one to the other when they need a break.'

'Three or four more days and then she'll be going home.'

'And she appreciates what you do for her.'

She tells me often enough, and she's always trying to slip ten-pound notes into my hand or my purse when she thinks I'm not looking. When she lets her guard down, the look in her eyes is tender and bewildered and she reaches out to touch my hand when I find her lost handbag or mislaid walking stick. But after days and days, even Mother Theresa would be losing patience.

The next morning, the three of us sit down together for breakfast. The smell of flaky croissants and fresh coffee fights the scent of lavender polish. A brand-new day full of possibilities and festive activities stretches out before us.

'After breakfast,' she says, turning towards me 'perhaps you can help me.'

'Don't say you need to write your Christmas cards. Don't say it.'

'Don't be silly, dear. I did those ages ago. Don't you remember?'

31. The Orchid

Despite my stumbling attempts to get to grips with Alex's situation, our relationship grew: a brief chat, a friendly smile or a comforting touch made me realise there was a two-way spark of interest. I needed to know more and she was happy to oblige. I hadn't planned to share my story with her yet, but that's what happened.

My second proper meeting with Alex was more like a tutorial than a chat. I had read all the pamphlets she'd given me and learned about the local intersex group she belonged to and what they did, but I still had questions. When she went all technical on me, speaking about X and Y chromosomes, naturally occurring variants and sex hormones, I zoned out a bit. My grade 'C' in human biology wasn't cutting it.

'But you have to understand the language,' she said, her voice rising in pitch and volume. 'You can't relate to people like me unless you take us seriously. You can't talk about sex and gender assignment, cisgender and trans as though the words all mean the same thing.'

I nodded, hoping my impression of thoughtful wisdom was convincing. We were sitting in the corner hugging the radiator. The November menu had been superseded by the Festive Christmas menu and the sugar lumps had been joined by a glass candleholder with tiny, painted, holly leaves dancing all the way round.

'What's it like now, forty years on? Is it still a problem?'

Alex laughed; a scornful, mocking laugh. Paused to sip her Latte.

'For me, you mean? Or for the world in general? Not that we like to think of ourselves as problems.'

I felt my cheeks reddening. She touched my arm reassuringly.

'Intersex births still happen, if that's what you mean, and it doesn't get much easier; but the stats are unreliable and unpalatable information is kept hidden under the radar. Almost 2% of people in the world have intersex traits. About the same number as those who have red hair.'

'We're both in minority groups, then.'

That was the first time I'd heard her laugh out loud. She beckoned to Gino to bring two more coffees.

'Even medics are ignorant and inexperienced because they don't see many cases but a child born with D.S.D . . . '

'D.S.D?'

'Disorders of Sexual Development. For goodness sake, didn't you read the pamphlet?'

I smiled my *I'm so sweet you can't be cross with me* smile. Expressing her frustration and laughing at my ineptitude were sure signs she was more comfortable with our relationship. As I was. A bit too comfortable, some might say.

'As I was saying, a child born with D.S.D. is less likely to be scooped off to theatre in the first few weeks though it still happens. Now they have gender committees and what they call *interdisciplinary conversations*. The individual is consulted about what they want. Revolutionary, huh? Who'd have thought.'

Determined to prove I had studied the literature she was keen to share with me, I flicked through the pages to a rather graphic image.

'But a decision has to be made, surely, when you can't determine the baby's gender?'

'Yeah. At the right time and for the right reasons.'

'I had no idea. . .'

She glared at me as though she were dealing with a gullible relative.

'Why would you? You're a vicar. You're not worldly. You live in the church, saying prayers and singing hymns. Everybody likes you.'

'Hah! I wish.'

Our conversation played on my mind over the next few days, keeping me awake at night. How dare anybody choose a gender for another human being? The next time we met, Luigi had hardly put the mugs down before I launched in. I wouldn't have won any prizes for listening skills but Alex had been away for Christmas and I'd been on a short break visiting college friends. I'd had too long to think about everything.

'I've been wondering. Were you saying last time you'd have preferred to be Alexander? That you're in the wrong skin?'

She shook her head, clutched her cup with one hand, and rearranged her fringe with the other.

'I'm comfortable with their choice, although others aren't as lucky. Looking like a girl and feeling like a girl are two completely different things.'

She picked up the New Year Specials menu and pretended to read.

'It's the fact I was seen as a freak and nobody waited to ask me what I wanted. That's what hurts.'

Sometimes, silence is the only helpful response.

'And that Mum and Dad were made to feel guilty and keep the real me a secret from close friends and family. You grow up being ashamed of yourself at a deep level without knowing why.'

We sat there, concentrating on our coffee while I resisted the urge to tell her my story. Priests are meant to keep proper boundaries, after all; not share their personal heartaches. Alex kept her eyes focused on her lap and took the tissue I handed her.

'Cry,' I said. 'Don't fight it.'

Eventually, she gave in.

'I tried churches. After forgiveness, I suppose. But one pastor told me my parents must have been sinful, and if I prayed more, I'd become a proper woman. It took me a long time to set foot inside a church again, let alone talk to anybody.'

'I don't blame you. What changed your mind?'

'I went to Auntie Gwen's funeral at the crematorium, last October, and you were in charge. The way you spoke about her, as though you knew her, as though she were worth the time and effort, made me think you might be different.'

'Well, I'm glad. Not that your Auntie Gwen died but because you had the guts to give me a chance.'

We continued to meet, on and off, for a few more months. February gave way to spring, and by late April we were able to sit outside, squashed against the stone wall, hoping nobody would need to escape from the pharmacy in a hurry. With a stretch of the imagination, we could have been on holiday in the Med. The table was covered with a red-checked cloth and the Easter Menu was decorated with yellow chicks and daffodils. A citrus smell wafted over the table when Gino offered us biscuits.

'New recipe. Lemon and poppy seeds. See what you think.'

Why did he always wink at me in that secretive way?

Alex told me about twelve-year-old Marian who was desperate to become Mark and who could have been Mark all along if a zealous surgeon hadn't removed his penis and given him hormone treatment. How she had wept uncontrollably when Julian had taken his own life the night before his eighteenth birthday, and how she'd shut herself in her bedroom for three days when she'd realized she would never be able to give birth. I'd coped with the same prospect for different reasons so we both railed against the God she said she didn't believe in. Finally, judging the moment was right, and blowing good practice guidelines to the wind, I told her my story – how I'd discovered in my first month at secondary school my dad wasn't my real dad. A bombshell which made me confused and ashamed, too.

'Suddenly, I found out the man I'd loved for eleven years had no genetic relationship with me whatsoever.'

'And if you'd known all along, you'd have coped.'

'I suppose. Hard to say. It was all excruciatingly embarrassing. Bad enough discovering your parents have had sex, but to learn Mum had done it with an old flame was all too much.'

'Your dad was amazing then. Staying with your mum and loving you. Never letting on you weren't his own.'

'Yeah. Mum had told him the minute she got home from her conference. Said it would never happen again, a moment of madness, too much to drink and all that crap. And then she discovered she was pregnant.'

Bethan reached for the lemon biscuit, brushing the poppy seeds off her lap.

'They'd been trying for a few months. They didn't know who the father was and tests weren't available then. They did one much later on but didn't tell me. It wouldn't have mattered, anyway. Dad said as soon as he held me in his arms, nothing would have forced him to let me go, wherever my genes had come from.

'Sweet. But telling you at the age when kids are getting hormonal and wondering who they are,' said Alex, twisting the napkin into a corkscrew. 'Wasn't great timing, was it?'

'No. At least I found out where my red hair came from.'

'Didn't you go looking for him when you were old enough? Your biological dad. Surely you wanted to meet him, find out more. You might have a troop of half brothers and sisters.'

'I was itching to do all that. Of course, I was. I told Dad I wasn't interested. That he was the only father I needed. I couldn't bear to make him suffer and I couldn't do it in secret. Too much goes on behind closed doors as it is. Anyway, Mum refused to tell me anything more while Dad was alive and he still is technically.'

'I assumed he'd died ages ago.'

'No. He's been in a specialist dementia unit for five years now. I've been begging Mum to tell me the truth for ages and now, the state she's in, I'm worried we've missed the boat.'

The sun was blazing down. Summer had arrived. I was there before her, sitting at the pavement table, moving the chairs into the shade, and checking out the Midsummer Feast menu. I half noticed a woman coming down the lane, striding out, a spring in her step, the green stems poking out at the top of a bag for life. I blinked and squinted into the sun. Alex?

'Love the hair,' I said, trying not to sound too surprised as I admired the professional cut and the peppery highlights. 'And the jacket.' The purple and silver orchid brooch was fixed firmly in place.

'Thanks. Thought it was time for a new image. Come out of hiding. Things have changed for me in the last few months and it's all down to you. I came to say thanks, and to tell you I can't see you for a while.'

'Oh.' I knew my face must have given away how deflated I was by the look on hers.

'Holiday? Work? Boyfriend?'

We had rarely spoken about other relationships, and her work, she'd said, was routine, part-time, accountancy, dead boring. Apart from agreeing open plan offices were the work of the devil, I had no idea what else she did when she wasn't having coffee with me.

'None of the above. I'm going to the States for four or five weeks. Doing all the tourist things. Then I'm going to confront the surgeon who mutilated me. Mr Armstrong. I've tracked him down.'

'Is that such a good idea?'

'God, Bethan, you're not my mother,' she said. 'Stop being a vicar for once.'

Not for the first time, I cursed the red hair and the way my blushes appeared without permission.

'He's willing to meet me but he won't let me record the interview. I know we can't change history and he isn't practising now but I need to see him face-to-face. Tell him why he was wrong. Tell him what effect he's had on his victims. And,' she paused, like a five-year-old with an exciting secret. 'Dad's coming with me. We've talked and talked, and I can see why he buried his head in the sand all those years.'

'Great news. About your dad.'

'Talking of which, I haven't stopped thinking about yours. And your mum.'

'Don't forget Armstrong will be surrounded by lawyers, protected up to the hilt.'

'OK. You don't want to talk about your family. Fair enough.'

I blushed, caught out in the act of denial.

'Doesn't matter about the lawyers. I don't want anything from Armstrong. I want to meet a human being who can persuade me he did his best at the time rather than the monster I've imagined him to be and then I can lay the ghost to rest.'

'I suppose that makes sense. You – you will be in touch when you're back?' Was I sounding too keen?

'Don't worry. You'll be the first to hear. I'll definitely be back. I've. . .' she paused, trying to flick the non-existent fringe. Her fingernails had grown back and I hadn't noticed.

'I've been elected chair of the regional intersex group. Start in September.'

'Amazing. Congratulations.'

'Decided I needed to take control rather than letting the past rule my life. We'll campaign, educate people through social media, visit universities and surgeries, write stuff and'

'Makes me exhausted just listening.'

'Well. The vision's great even if it is a bit ambitious. Anything's better than nothing, not that you can achieve much with fifteen people and a few hangers-on.'

'Could I be a hanger-on?' I said, without thinking. 'I mean, what about letting the church be involved?'

'I was hoping you'd say that. That's why I bought you this.'

She pulled her tote bag from behind her chair and manoeuvred a delicate plant onto the table. It was an orchid. Like the brooch. Though it wasn't purple and silver.

'I don't want you to forget me. You *did* know the orchid's the Intersex emblem, didn't you? Don't tell me you didn't read that bit either?'

'Of course, I did,' I lied, my cheeks reddening again.

'I'm planning a symposium on the eighth of November and wondered if we could use St Jude's as a venue.'

'And call it The Other Remembrance Day or Who do you think I am?' Sometimes I surprised myself with my brilliance. 'Central, well-connected, lots of community links . . .'

'And adorable, friendly vicar,' she said. 'Red hair and all.'

32. The Fountain Pen

Coping with death is manageable when you are a professional but not so easy when the tables are turned and you're the one having to let go when all you want to do is cling on. That's what it was like for Isaac, me and Mum as we managed the final few days.

Isaac and I grabbed what time we could to sort out Mum's things. Half a day here, a couple of hours there. In between work and sitting and waiting and spooning ice cream. Dad was in a world of his own, Mum was never coming home and we were keen to push on before winter set in. She wouldn't miss the broken ladder, paint cans or myriad pots, buckets and rusty tools. Joyce was an inheritor of her parents' wartime austerity. If you saw anything in the shops, you snapped it up while you had the chance. You kept everything *for a rainy day*. Stubs of pencils, bits of paper held together with bulldog clips, perished rubber bands. And, alongside these bits of domestic detritus were precious, irreplaceable items. Black and white photographs, a swan-shaped brooch, and letters tied with ribbon.

Some things cried out to be kept, like the tiny pair of metal spectacles stuffed at the back of a drawer in Dad's bedside table with a note in Mum's faint handwriting: *Charlie's glasses, aged 18 months.* They must have cost a fortune. No NHS in those days. There were paintings with my nephews' awkward handwriting, all dated and folded carefully. People with huge faces and no bodies on faded sugar paper.

I found a picture of me lying on a rug in the garden in a hideous knitted outfit with Mum sitting beside me. On the back written in the same feint writing, *Bethan, three months old*. How did Dad manage, standing behind the camera, knowing the child in front of him wasn't his? How could my mother have put him through that? How could she have allowed it to happen in the first place? Tears turned into sobs. I threw myself face-down onto the bed and let the emotions take over for a few minutes. Then I remembered Isaac could come in at any minute. I wiped my face on my sleeve and stuffed the photo in my pocket.

There were more pictures of Isaac in a sailor suit, his eyes closed against the sun despite the frilly canopy over his pram. I was bending over him, on tiptoe, shaking a rattle while our father gazed at us with a beatific smile. He did look as if he loved us both. What a saint he must have been.

The fountain pen was in the zip pocket of Mum's faux leather shoulder bag, buried under crumpled tissues and till receipts. I might have missed it if I hadn't felt through the lining, still in a black leather pouch and in immaculate condition. I gasped. I still used a fountain pen but this was in a different league. It looked like a genuine Mont Blanc. I considered myself a bit of an expert since I'd seen a T.V. crime documentary where a whole consignment had been swapped for fakes. Of course, comparisons were tricky if you've never handled a genuine item, but this pen had quality. If it was an imitation, it was first-rate. It felt solid, the iconic, white, mountain snow was clear on the cap top and the nib was slim and delicate, perfect for Mum's light touch. But the colours of the lid – yellow, black, blue, orange – seemed out of keeping with her more usual taste for blues and greens.

The receipt, dated 8th December 2017, declared this was a special edition inspired by the *Sergeant Pepper* album. Really? Mum could sing along with 'Lucy in the Sky' or 'When I'm Sixty-Four', but she wasn't a die-hard groupie. Anyway, she would never have splashed out on herself; not for a fountain pen. It must have been a gift. A very generous and unusual gift.

Tucked inside the case was a card, saying *Remember when*. Remember when what? Surely she was being honest about the one-night stand or was this evidence that their marriage had always been a charade? Tenth December 2017 was her seventy-fifth birthday. A Sunday. I remember rushing off after church so we'd have time to visit Dad before going out to lunch.

'Charlie, your wife and your children have come to visit you.'

Charlie had frowned, looked us up and down and said, 'I don't have a wife. I may have had a son. I never had a daughter.' He had turned his face away.

'Don't take it to heart,' said the carer. 'It's the illness talking. Not your dad.' We kissed him anyway. Isaac knelt to hug him before the nurse tucked in his blanket and wheeled him away.

We would have chosen a more upmarket restaurant for her birthday lunch, but Mum had gone on about familiarity being important at her age and needing to be sure there was good wheelchair access and clean toilets. Isaac and I had ordered flowers to be delivered on the tenth of every month for a year. I remember Robbie, his son, saying she'd better not die before the year was over. Smiling at the memories, I put the pen in my bag along with the spectacles. I would check with Isaac later when he arrived with his trailer.

'Never seen it before,' he said when I showed him. 'Mum had dozens of pencils and biros in every room. Nothing like this, though.'

'It's garish,' I said, unscrewing and screwing the lid. 'Not Mum's thing at all. And the timing's all wrong. Sergeant Pepper was over fifty years ago.'

'Keep it though. Might be worth a bit.'

How would my mother have taken herself to s jeweller's shop in the middle of town and why would she have bought such an expensive item? Who had written the cryptic *'remember when.'* Every life had its secrets, I knew that better than most. But Mum?

A few days later, I excused myself from the deanery synod meeting and bell-ringers' AGM to sit with Mum. It wasn't much of a sacrifice. They weren't the highlights of the church's calendar and the opportunities to be with Mum were fast fading. She was beyond the stage of having lucid conversations about pens.

'I've been thinking,' said Mum, every word an effort. 'I need to ask you a question.'

Would this be the great reveal? Would I learn my father's name at the eleventh hour? Might there be a secret half-sibling? My heart beat more insistently.

'What's that Mum?' I held my breath, strained to catch the words.

'All this extra food I'm eating, all this ice cream. Who's going to pay?'

I smiled. Stroked her hand.

'It's fine. We can afford the ice cream.

Everything's all right. Think of it as an all-inclusive holiday. You can let go now, Mum. I'll look after Dad and Isaac.'

Two days later, when we stepped out of the room for a moment while the carers freshened her up, she let go and slipped away, traces of ice cream still visible on her chin.

33. The Funeral

I know it was months ago, Michael, but I haven't felt strong enough to write about the funeral until now. I hope you've got a pot of coffee or a bottle of wine as you're in for a long story! Gavin, my first vicar, took the funeral. I wanted to do it myself, to be in control but first Isaac and then Gavin persuaded me not to be stubborn.

'You're the grieving daughter,' said Gavin. 'You can't be the professional as well.' I'm grateful I listened to him. It was strange being on the other side of the fence, sitting in the front row instead of standing behind the lectern. People always tell me the service passes in a haze. You can't remember a thing anybody says but you do remember the feelings, the emotions, the atmosphere, the sounds and the smells. They were right.

Mum hadn't wanted a church service. Said she felt hypocritical since she only attended when she came with me. It would be a small affair, she'd said, so we were surprised by how many people came, given her age. Even more surprised that the crematorium refurbishment was tasteful and not depressing and dowdy like the old one, with its uncomfortable chairs and tatty curtains. There was an etched window from floor to ceiling that flooded the chapel with light but it was a place for all faiths and none, so there were no visible Christian symbols. The funeral director had to ask for the cross to be brought from the store cupboard.

I always tell grieving families that past losses might come to the fore when they attend any other funeral. A miscarriage, the loss of a child, a friend, a sibling or a parent no matter how long ago. Forewarned was forearmed, I said. Hah! Easy to say when you're the vicar but not as easy to cope with when it's your mother in the coffin. Strange to be the one with the mountain of tissues in your pocket and to be thrown by the sight of the coffin. I wasn't only grieving for my mother. I was hit by a wave of sadness for Dad at the nursing home, in his locked-in world, unaware of who Mum was, let alone that she'd died; for all the lost children. For Tom, Tammy, Ben and Tyler. And, I realized at just the wrong moment, for my eleven-year-old self on the day she lost her identity.

As we sang 'Lord of all hopefulness, Lord of all joy, whose trust ever childlike no cares could destroy', I wanted to shout what about *my* trust? That was destroyed. In one sudden revelation. Of course, I didn't shout anything of the sort. I sang through the tears to the end of the final verse 'Be there at our sleeping and give us, we pray, your peace in our hearts, Lord, at the end of the day.' I craved that kind of peace to get through this overwhelming tiredness. I'd give a lot for a tiny bit of peace.

Isaac and I didn't speak properly until after lunch. Luckily, we'd opted for a buffet so the extra numbers weren't a problem. Hope you appreciated the *good wheelchair access and clean toilets*. We were laughing, a bit unkindly perhaps, about the two remaining members of the afternoon reading group who couldn't read large print books, let alone the service sheet. Funny how grief affects your sense of humour. We remembered, too, why we only ever saw our cousins at weddings and funerals. We were glad to see the last of them drifting off, duty done. And then there was you.

I'd registered your presence when we walked in behind the coffin, but I was too distracted and tied up with polite niceties. We were finishing the dregs of the coffee before I asked Isaac who you were. Almost everybody else had gone.

'Who's the odd guy sitting by the radiator?' I asked him. 'The frail, thin one with the check scarf.'

Isaac didn't know either but he'd spotted the classic Austin Riley in the car park and the real live chauffeur with a peaked cap reading the paper. I could tell he was impressed so I pretended to be, too. Something about you was familiar. I see dozens of people and forget whether I've met them at a wedding or a christening but you were different. Like I knew you but couldn't quite place you.

'I'll go and say hello, then,' I said.

You were taciturn and awkward, as though you might be an unwelcome guest, imposing on a family affair. Your legs were long and thin and you were clinging to your hat like a security blanket, looking around nervously for an escape route, but then lots of people do that when they see a vicar approaching.

'I hope you don't mind my coming,' you said. I was struck by how well-spoken and well-groomed you were. 'Forgive me for not getting up.'

'Any friend of Mum's is very welcome. I don't think we've met, have we?'

'No,' you said. 'We haven't. I'm Michael.'

I waited, racking my brains. Michael? Michael who?

'I knew your mother when we were younger.' He blushed, swizzled the hat in his hand, and looked directly at me as though he were weighing up what to say.

'In fact, we were in love with one another.'

Well, don't hold back, I wanted to say. Tell it like it is. It's only my mother's funeral. Nothing important. Instead, I think I laughed, a nervous kind of laugh. Eventually, when I realized you were serious, I managed to stutter 'When? What went wrong?'

'She was still a teenager. We wanted to get married but Joyce's father didn't approve,' you said. You weren't good enough for his daughter, you had no money, were a few years older than her and she wasn't brave enough to run away.

'And you kept in touch with her all these years?'

'No. not at all. Not even Christmas cards. We knew it was wrong. Then, by chance, and honestly it was by chance, we met at a residential charities' conference. Must be nearly forty years ago.'

I knew when you looked away, lost in the memory of the event, that the meeting had been significant.

'After my wife died, I searched for your mother through *Friends Reunited*. I wasn't sure what was more surprising – that I found her or that we'd both learnt how to work the technology!'

I was pleased you'd seen the announcement in *The Times* and come. You said you were glad you'd taken the risk, and so relieved to meet me that words poured out like you'd been saving them up for years. I pulled up a chair next to you. Something was clicking into place but I couldn't quite grasp it. Anybody watching would have thought I was drunk. You asked if I'd seen a ghost and said that funerals were always stressful.

Had you met Mum again, I asked, anticipating the answer. Yes, you'd said, as I expected. Just once. You'd always remembered her birthday and a couple of years ago, you'd invited her out for lunch. Your chauffeur had driven you. You bought her a fountain pen. A Montblanc. *Sergeant Pepper*. Like me and Isaac, you'd thought it was a strange choice but she'd fallen in love with it at the jewellers. Said it reminded her of wilder times. Mum was always full of surprises.

Then you went all lyrical on me saying it was a special edition pen and she was special to you, even though you'd lived most of your lives apart. How she'd brought colour into your life when there wasn't any. It was no more than a silly extravagance. I didn't think it was a silly extravagance at all.

We sat together in silence for five minutes or more. Do you remember? Trying not to notice the tears in each other's eyes. I was fuming about my grandfather standing in the way of love. Yet, if he hadn't, I wouldn't be here now, nor Isaac. Except, maybe I *would* have been here. Was it possible that you, with your posh car and tailored suit, were. . .

I knocked those thoughts on the head and scrabbled around in my bag to find the pen which I offered back to you. Mum would have wanted that. You pulled a perfectly laundered, white handkerchief from your pocket and blew your nose. Without thinking, I asked if you'd write to me and Isaac and tell us what you were doing, and more about what you and Mum got up to – well, maybe not *all* the details. You'd laughed. Out of the blue, you said 'Your mother had such an infectious laugh. Did you know Isaac means laughter?'

'And Bethan means *pledged to God*,' I said, realising I rather resented that. I didn't want to be *pledged to God*. I wanted to be loved by my family, know who I was, and find my own soulmate. God could have his share but not all of me. You understood what I was thinking, saw my discomfort, annoyance, whatever. You sensed what I needed without being told.

'I think your parents were kind and caring people, who loved you and Isaac very much. I'll take the pen, for now.' You took it from me like it was the most precious thing in the world and you would guard it with your life. I knew then we could trust you, and that you had loved Mum enough to let her go.

'I'm going travelling soon,' you said. 'Only in the UK. Revisiting favourite places. I'm not sure how long for. I'll send you postcards, and I'll use the fountain pen. And I will tell my children that when I die, they must give it back. That way, you will never forget me.'

34. The Engagement Ring

For some people, their final years are an opportunity to live life to the full, despite the infirmities which turn up like unwelcome guests. Bishop's Place provided a safe environment for navigating the future, dealing with the past and living in the present.

'I wish the beeper would stop buzzing long enough for me to drink my coffee,' said Audrey as she let Bethan in. 'I'm easily distracted and you can't be too careful.'

After eight weeks at Bishop's Place, she knew most of the friends and relatives, but there were still strangers and newcomers. Bethan sympathised with the problem. The last time she'd visited, Barbara, one of the new residents, had slipped through the half-open door behind her with a careless wave. Coat-tailing, it was called. Bishop's Place wasn't a prison. It was a home-from-home like the brochure said, but some people needed protecting. Like Audrey's own mother who had moved from Eastbourne a few days before and couldn't recognise her daughter, let alone negotiate the outside world. And Isobel, who was content while she was writing endless cards to imaginary friends but would go to pieces outside on her own.

'Do you find it hard coming in here?' said Audrey. 'Remembering your mum and all those hours you spent with her at the end? And with your dad still in Ridgemount.'

'Thanks. It's fine. It's my job. I have to come. Who would take the service if it wasn't me? Anyway, I can't believe how well you look, and what a difference you're making here.'

Audrey flicked through the pages of her day book, blushed.

'I'm grateful for your help with the restraining order, Bethan. I'd never have thought of it myself. Wouldn't have had a clue.'

'Roger was the real brains,' said Bethan. He's a trustee and knew what to do. He had the idea first.'

'But you gave me a reference and that counted, too. I will be eternally grateful. Eliza Bradley would like a chat before the service, by the way. Her and William, the army guy.'

Bethan laughed. 'The army guy! He was a brigadier, stars and all.'

'Well, whatever he was, Faye says he and Eliza have become quite chummy. You wouldn't think they'd have anything in common, would you?'

'Then there's Barbara. She's a dark horse. There's a story there for sure, not that it's any of my business. I think she's a troubled soul.'

Bethan knocked on Eliza's door. Eliza and Billy were sharing a Madeira cake and a pot of tea. Around them, photos of Joe and Greg, Caitlin and the grandchildren took centre stage. Eliza had used bright cushions and embroidered table mats to make the room her own. And she had put on weight thought Bethan, unlike Billy, who was more of a skeleton than a body. A skeleton tucked under a tartan blanket.

'Forgive me for not getting up. It goes against the grain to remain seated in the presence of a padre.'

Eliza smoothed his blanket and laid her hand over his.

'I've told Billy all about Sara,' she said.

'That's good,' said Bethan looking to Billy for a response.

'I had no idea. We were young. A bit reckless. I would have . . .'

'We've both had happy marriages,' said Eliza 'and interesting children. We don't regret a thing but we've got friendly again since I moved in.'

'And we want to ask you, Padre, if you will conduct our wedding. In church.'

'As soon as you can,' said Eliza. 'We may not have long together.'

'Can you believe it?' said Faye as she walked with Bethan to the door, when the weekly service was over. 'What a turn-up. Dad and Eliza. After all these years. I was lost for words when they told me. First that they knew each other at all, and then about the baby, and when they showed me the engagement ring, well, I burst into tears.'

'And what did Titus have to say?'

'About the engagement? Or the fact that the remains of his half-sister are buried a few metres away from his mother's ashes? I got in first. Told him to be grateful. Dad's already had two more years than we expected. And look at him now. He won't have long, but his last weeks will be happy. I think he feels he needs to make amends, though he never knew Eliza was pregnant. He'd never have left her to fend for herself. Not if she'd told him. Anyway, I'll always be glad we talked him out of a trip to Switzerland.'

'I bet he is, too. How about Eliza's son, Greg and his family? Must have been a shock for them.'

'They're fine about it. Lizzie says she's got more material for her degree project, whatever that is.

'Should I visit Barbara, the new resident?'

'Not if you value your life. She's a prickly one. Doesn't like interruptions. She spends hours on her mobile phone. No idea who she's talking to at all hours of the day.'

35. The Breakdown

Life wasn't fair, thought Bethan, as she drove home. It was messy and complicated. Pathos and pain jostled alongside joy and love. Living and dying were both difficult, and you never knew when you were getting things right and when you were storing up trouble for yourself or somebody else. A moment of passion, a baby born too soon, a word spoken at the wrong time, a debilitating illness. One event, one mistake could change the course of a person's life and others who got caught in the crossfire. John Donne was right. Nobody is an island. No man or woman.

And now, to cap it all, at the end of a draining day, she had to proofread the service sheet for the annual memorial service.

Thanksgiving for all those we have loved and lost, she read on the front page. The list expanded every year. Some people wanted whole tranches of names read out, going back years. It was unwieldy and annoying but not a battle she was willing to fight. They might be lighting candles all evening, but so what? She glanced at the names. Some had died after a long and happy life. Pru Wainwright, Joe and Keziah, her own mother. They'd had their three score years and ten and often a good many more. And some hadn't They were the tragedies, the deaths out of season, the deaths which shouldn't have happened at all, not if there was a God who loved them. Baby Benjamin, Tyler, Tom and Paul, Louis and Sara Eliza. Amelia, Tammy and, at Harriet's insistence *all the other children who have died violent deaths.* And what about the elephants in the room, she asked herself. What about Father Dominic and Keith, the car dealer? How shall we remember them?'

The clanging of the phone disturbed her. Couldn't they leave her alone for one evening? She pushed KitKat off her lap, yanked the mobile out of her bag and punched the green button.

'Yes?' she spat out.

'Reverend Davies? Bethan?' said the surprised voice. 'It's about your father. I think you need to come.'

Bethan sat rooted to the armchair gazing into the middle distance. She knew she had to get to Ridgemount in a hurry and that there was little time to lose. She knew that required making her limbs move and engaging her brain. The intention was one thing, doing it was another. She had no idea how to achieve an impossible task. Her body refused to obey instructions and her mind was clogged up like a pile of tangled wool. What had just happened? Why was she sitting here feeling sad and empty? Somebody was dying but she couldn't for the life of her remember who.

She vaguely recalled telling the woman on the phone she would contact Isaac but who was Isaac? Did she know any Isaacs? There was an Isaac in the bible but it couldn't be him. She grabbed her mobile. Somewhere there was a contact list. Maybe he was in there. After three false starts, she spotted the telephone symbol and scrolled down but couldn't find him. She was being tricked by a strange woman. Was the caller a woman? She sounded like a woman but could have been a man. She couldn't be expected to remember everything. She jumped when the back door slammed.

'Who's there?' She stood up and stepped towards the voice. 'You can't come in. Leave me alone.'

'Bethan?' Alex nudged the door open with her foot, holding the Indian takeaway bag under her arms. 'Oh my God. What's happened?'

'Don't you talk to me about God. I'm through with God. Sod God! Hah! that rhymes.'

Alex put the curry in the kitchen. Walked slowly back into the room and taking Bethan's arm, guided her towards the basket chair.

'Come and sit down. Take a deep breath. Tell me what's happened.'

Bethan sat, staring straight ahead.

'Where am I? There was a call. Ages ago. Telling me I had to go home but I *am* home. Who are you?'

Alex took Bethan's mobile and checked the recent calls. She dialled the number. 'Ridgemount Nursing Home. How may I help you?' All Bethan could hear was a burble of voices. She didn't have the energy to fight anymore. She folded her hands in her lap, closed her eyes and blanked out the world.

'Bethan. Look at me. It's me. Alex. I'm going to ring Isaac and then we're going to ask Roger to come and take us to see your dad. He's very ill and you need to be there.'

Isaac was on speed dial. He would leave immediately. Roger arrived within minutes and, despite Bethan's deadpan expression and robotic behaviour, they persuaded her into the back of his BMW. Setting aside his respect for the law, Roger covered the twenty miles in record time, exchanging concerned looks with Alex. Neither of them dared to voice their fears.

'I'm very pleased you made it, Bethan,' said the carer who met them in the hallway. 'Your brother's with your father. He's not got long.'

'What's the rush? Why hasn't he got long?' The carer hesitated, raised an eyebrow at Roger. Roger shook his head. 'It's your father, Bethan,' said Roger. 'You remember. He's been here for a while now. You need to go and say goodbye before he dies.'

'Dies? Dies? What's wrong with him? Why is everybody dying? I'll never know who I am now. There'll be nobody left to tell me.' They led her up the stairs and into the room. When Isaac stood up, tears streaming down his face, she relaxed. She knew exactly who he was.

'Isaac. Thank goodness you're here. I couldn't find you on my phone. Somebody's dying but they won't tell me who or why.'

Charlie took his last breath with his children sitting on either side of his bed. Alex and Roger hovered outside the door, concerned about how Bethan might react. In the end, she just sat still stroking his hand and whispering to him. Eventually, the doctor arrived to confirm what they all knew had happened.

'You did this,' Bethan spat at the unsuspecting doctor, who glanced at Isaac nervously for enlightenment. 'You did this. You killed our mum and now you've finished off our dad and I'll see that you pay.'

'Come on, love,' said Alex. 'Let's go home. We'll talk about it tomorrow. Say goodbye to your father.'

36. Under the Oak Tree

The oak tree was there when the story began and was still there at the end, a symbol of faithfulness and stability.

Bethan noticed how many changes had occurred during the year she'd been away, especially in the garden. Somebody had mown the uneven lawn and weeded the gaps between the paving stones, the shrubs were coming to life, a few already in full blossom. The clematis was growing freely up the drainpipe by the back door and irises stood to attention against the back wall. It had never been this pretty and inviting.

Of course, the oak tree was there with an abundance of wavy, emerald leaves and nestled underneath, half a metre from the trunk, was a new bench underneath which KitKat was curled up asleep. She read the small, brass plaque: *Bethan's bench.* She breathed the fresh air deep into her lungs, felt the touch of the sun on her cheeks and listened to the birds busy with twigs in the beech hedge. The geese were honking loudly as they landed on the pond. She stood for a moment, glad to be home. Indoors, she kicked off her shoes, filled the kettle and flicked the switch. Next to the teapot was a heap of post and a white card was top of the pile.

'Dear Bethan,' she read. 'We hope you don't mind but we've been tidying things ready for your return. We can't wait to see you at church again. We've missed you. The interim vicar was fine, but she wasn't you. Flapjacks are in the cake tin, milk in the fridge and ready meals on the top shelf of the freezer. You won't forget the summer fair meeting, will you? Love Magda, Audrey and Fiona.'

Another postcard, with a picture of St Jude's on the front, bore the simple message. *I hope you enjoy the bench. Welcome home. Roger.*

'Odd, isn't it,' she said to Alex later as they polished off a cassoulet. 'I've been away for a year, yet it's like I've never left.'

'Except the garden's tidier and the flowers are blooming.'

'The parish has survived without me. I'm not sure whether to be pleased or disappointed. Even the bishop has sent a welcome home card. Or his PA has. Most importantly, I know who I am and what I want.'

'Back to life and back to work, then? Back to normal. As we were?'

Bethan shifted her weight from one foot to the other.

'I didn't say *that.*'

It was Alex's turn to look hesitant. She raised her eyebrows. Waited.

'Michael's coming to stay next week.'

Alex nodded. 'I can move out for a few days if you like. I don't want to be in the way.'

'You know he's my genetic father.'

'Of course. What's that got to do with anything?' Bethan could hear from her voice Alex was getting impatient.

'I want him to be the first to know. Can I tell him I've asked you to marry me and you've said Yes?'

37. Dearest Michael

How wonderful to see you again and share that long, lazy lunch. I can't believe it's only a year since we first clapped eyes on each other. A lot has happened since then. I was going to say I feel like I've known you all my life, but that would be too corny. Thank goodness you got to see the consultant in time. You're certainly making the most of being in remission, and I'm glad you liked the Fitbit. It must be a huge relief to discover you're good for a few more years when you thought your days were numbered. You call yourself *reconditioned*; I might say *resurrected*. I feel like that, too. And thank you for being so welcoming to Alex. It means so much to me that you like her.

The river Itchen looks gentle and sedate in your latest postcard. All that chalky water and brown trout. I'm glad you're still sending me cards and still using the fountain pen you gave Mum for her birthday. We're like a kind of lonely hearts' club band aren't we, you and me? I bet Paul McCartney would be surprised how important *Sergeant Pepper* was to an octogenarian father and his gay, mixed-up daughter. Though not quite as mixed up now.

The chaplaincy came to an end. I loved every minute, especially the chance to write. I'll never stop writing now. I'm determined to make time for writing now. I'll scribble away in between weddings and funerals and all the other stuff. I was back in St Jude's in time for Easter. An apt festival, wouldn't you say, what with all the talk of resurrection and new life? Maybe a dose of unfettered joy and power will invigorate me, too. I wonder what you've made of my writing and what you make of my life. Did I get the mood and the details right in *The Funeral*?

As you can see, the stories are a mixed bag. I've been as honest as I can be in my personal stories. As for the others, they are all true, too, in their own way, but I've used my imagination and had to put myself in the shoes of comparative strangers. The timescales are a bit random and the stories aren't in the exact order they happened because that's how ministry is. You're given snippets of information, off-the-cuff revelations and random comments. People only tell you what they want you to know when they choose.

I decided to write one or two in the first person so I could inhabit the heads of the people involved. It was me losing Paul, me grieving the loss of Ellen, me dying with Tom. Oddly, I couldn't write about my breakdown in that way because when it all happened, I was the outsider, watching from the sidelines. Why am I being defensive and apologetic? If I've learned nothing else, I should have learned to be more confident.

Whenever I read the stories, I realise how intertwined the lives of individuals are. I don't quite believe that when a butterfly flaps its wings on the banks of the Amazon, it affects us in Swannery, but you get the picture. I'm glad you're coming to stay soon. We've got to make up for the best part of forty years before I'm bogged down again in the next tranche of living and dying, and you, well, you've got a new daughter to add to your family. A whole lot more trouble, you might be thinking!

I think we've both learned the hard way to make the most of every moment, to understand that letting go is the way forward. I wish I could say I've forgiven Mum for not telling me about you, but it ... it's more like I've come to terms with it. I suppose it was her way of staying loyal to Dad, but nothing can hurt him now. I'm surprised by how much I miss her and then, in a heartbeat, it all changes, and I'm cross with her again. They should have told me. You can't keep such vital secrets, but I'm gradually letting go of the bitterness. After all, I tell other people to do that all the time. Forgive, be thankful, and embrace life. Sermon over! Almost!

Dad's death was the end of a long chapter of my life. I can just about remember saying goodbye to him just before he took his last breath, sitting beside him and stroking his hand as I did with Mum. I don't know if he heard us, but I like to think he did. I can't believe Alex and Roger got me into the car and to his bedside in time. Alex said I was using words she didn't think I knew, beyond embarrassing. The doctor said I was exhibiting signs of an extreme form of stress reaction. The body shuts down when the mind has had enough, and all the usual filters disappear. I'm going with his version.

I've forgiven God for not being the God I'd invented. Given up thinking I can explain everything and have faith all sewn up in a watertight box. I wanted God to be the perfect father with neat answers for every eventuality and no loose ends. I was desperate to explain to Verity and Louise, Harriet and Roger, and all the others why God hadn't charged in on a white horse and rescued their loved ones. Now I know I can live with blurred edges and uncertainty, and I've stopped searching for perfection. When I look in the mirror, I can see Mum, Dad, and bits of you, and my life makes sense. Let's hope the world is ready for the new me.

Love, Bethan

Acknowledgements

Thanks to L.V.Matthews, the author of several psychological thrillers, who gave helpful advice and encouragement; to Gary Dalkin, and Sophie Beal and Rachel Theunissen of Cadence Publishing who worked with me on early versions; to the staff at York Publishing Services.

Book Club Questions

Letting Go One of the recurring themes of the book is *Letting Go*. The characters are compelled to let go of loved ones, past hurts, arguments, ambition or life itself.

How far does this theme resonate with you?

Children Fertility and infertility, raising children, adopting or losing them are deep issues which are well represented throughout the novel. Which story concerning children was most moving?

Siblings Sibling relationships can be complex. The dynamics can be exciting and interesting, dangerous and difficult. Which siblings make the most progress in their relationship?

Forgiveness Harbouring resentment and bearing grudges adversely affect the person who cannot forgive, and the one who remains unforgiven. Which characters inspire you most in the way they learned to forgive and/or be forgiven?

Growing Old The UK population is getting older. This is both a blessing and a curse for living longer does not always imply living well. How do you feel about the way the elderly are presented in the novel?

Bereavement Being born is the first experience of loss because the baby is forced to give up the safety of the womb for the insecurity of the world. Everybody will experience loss, and there are many examples in the book. Who has the best strategy for surviving loss?

Names Names are important in this novel: choosing them, owning them, living with them. Does any of this resonate with you as you consider your name or the names you have chosen for others?